May 1, 2016.

Hi Kristi,
Happy Reading and.
Best Wishes.

THE SUITABLE
INHERITOR

Thank you

D1714083

BY PUSHPENDRA
MEHTA

Author of Win the Battles
of Life & Relationships and
Tomorrow's Young Achievers

Pushpendra Mehta

To

God, for the gift of writing you gave me.

My mom and dad, Nirmala and Vijay, and my siblings, Malini and Sher, for encouraging me to write to make a difference in people's lives. Your timely reminders to keep writing have made me embrace words as a journey of self-discovery and self-expression.

My partner, my soul, and my wife, Madhur, for sharing my passions for reading and writing that made it possible for me to chase a dream of writing my first novel.

ONE

A few days ago I was stirred up out of deep sleep by an uncharacteristic dream—a lady dressed in white led me to the beautiful Pacific Ocean and whispered in my ear, "The ethereal ocean will now bring a wave of graces your way. Keep your inner door open to receive the special graces and discover your true destiny." I had never seen such an overwhelmingly attractive woman in my life. A pity we met in a dream and our walk to the Pacific Ocean lasted only a few minutes. She disappeared mysteriously, and I frantically searched for her in all directions, but in vain. My desperation woke me up, only to find my apartment in Chicago engulfed in darkness. It was the early hours of the morning, and even the lights in my home needed rest.

The enigmatic woman who appeared in my dream subliminally resurfaced while I was flying to Peru, evoking within me an inexplicable feeling that she and I would meet soon. That instinct got far more intense as my flight descended on Jorge Chávez International Airport in Lima at 8:30 p.m.

Christened by its Spanish founders as the City of Kings, Lima struck me as a very clean city. I had been told it never rains in Lima. The weather was perfect, neither hot nor cold. As a cab drove me through the city, the metropolis appeared as a cluster of small towns.

Never had I scrutinized a city that I was visiting for the first time with the precision of a highly skilled surgeon. It was as if my inner voice was nudging me to scan every street in search of the attractive woman in white who would somehow take me closer to my destiny. My rational mind believed otherwise and termed her as a figment of imagination. A trip to Latin America can conjure a sense of the mystical, however, and my hunch would not give up. *It will happen in Lima*, that inner voice said. *Such things do not only happen in the movies.*

Between the battle of the heart and the mind, I didn't realize the cab had traversed the distance from the airport to the venue of my stay, Del Pilar Miraflores Hotel.

"Mr. Elliott, welcome to Del Pilar Hotel. I hope you enjoyed the drive from the airport," said the charming lady at the reception desk. She had a lovely smile and seemed fluent in English. A quick glance at her name badge and I knew how to address her: Andrea Gonzales.

"Yes, indeed. Thank you, Andrea. I'm hoping to explore more of Lima during the next few days." I was trying to be polite, even though I was utterly exhausted after the long flight. Andrea was perceptive enough to notice my fatigue, and expeditiously provided me the card to my room with a complimentary coupon for a pisco sour, the national drink of Peru and considered among the finest cocktails in the world. The exquisite drink's origin had been in dispute—was it from Peru or Chile? But there was no question that I was pleased with the opportunity to taste the authentic drink that was created with Pisco—a regional brandy—lemon juice, egg whites, simple syrup, and regional bitters.

My room was on the sixth floor and was as cozy as the nest of a bird. Access to Internet was free. This mattered to me the most. In a digital economy, man has a new master—technology—and I could not do without my omnipresent companions: social media and e-mail. I was tempted to check my e-mails right then, but after an exhausting flight, slumber is as precious as a pretty woman's enchanting touch.

It was 10:00 p.m. I decided to skip dinner and hit the sack, only to wake up twelve hours later. I had a meeting at noon, but there was enough time before that to see if there was a Starbucks in the vicinity. I have a fetish for their classic chai tea latte. The clerk at the reception desk told me that the closest Starbucks was barely five minutes away by foot. That was sufficient to get my adrenaline pumping, as the aroma of chai tea lured me all the way to Starbucks.

At twelve, I was greeted by Andrew Smith in the lobby of the hotel. "Michael, it is a pleasure to meet you. Thank you for accepting my invitation of coming to Lima. My clients are looking forward to your words of wisdom. They know you are highly sought after these days."

Andrew was nearly sixty and yet looked no older than early forties. He was tall, handsome, and broad shouldered. I already knew some of the keys to his striking looks and personality—he exercised vigorously, meditated deeply, and ate appropriately.

I had read an article about Andrew that called him "The Adonis Who Repairs Relationships." The published piece explained how Andrew's good looks, compassionate disposition, glib style of communicating, penchant for meditation, and healthy food made him the ideal relationship coach.

"Thank you for inviting me," I replied. "It is truly an honor to be in your presence. You have had an enormous impact in the lives and relationships of tens of thousands of people."

I liked the way we shook hands. His body language was positive and his grip firm. Never did he take his eyes off me. He had relocated from Chicago to Lima two years earlier, and had over the last four years built up a thriving relationship-coaching enterprise that boasted of a big clientele base across the Americas and Europe.

Andrew had invited me to Lima to speak to his younger clients on important attributes that influenced success in professional and personal relationships. I discovered later that this was a pretext. At the time he was exploring the possibility of finding a worthy successor. He wanted to hand the baton of his business to an upcoming and credible relationship coach, who exemplified sensitivity toward varied cultures and demographics, believed in continual learning and change, and, more importantly, whose target audience was young minds. He believed, as did I, that it's the young who can best shape the destiny of a nation. Andrew was looking to share his success with a suitable relationship coach, and apparently he had set his eyes on me as a possible worthy heir.

I ran a very successful relationship-coaching venture for young minds in Chicago, or so Andrew thought. This was partially correct. My advisory service was up-and-coming, and had received most of its clients through a reporter's glowing review about my work, which was featured in a prominent Chicago newspaper. Andrew had erroneously assumed the complimentary media coverage was an indicator of a hugely successful coaching practice. But things aren't always exactly what they seem. Publicity and word-of-mouth marketing can sometimes conceal reality and make a fairly successful business venture appear gargantuan.

I had been overwhelmed and ecstatic when he wrote to invite me to address his young clients. An invitation from him would attract the attention of prominent media companies, leading to big-time fame. He was providing a golden opportunity for me to define my career and turn my moment in the sun into a permanent stay. Paradoxically, I was also entertaining the pretentious thought that Andrew needed my insights, that I had something special to offer him. As if this was not enough, a few days after I received his invitation, I inanely began to cast aspersions on his motive of inviting me to Lima. Why would a mega-relationship adviser waste his precious time over a puny competitor? Was I truly a competitor? I told myself to be vigilant, that forewarned was forearmed, and yet I knew that a one-on-one meeting with him could be one of the greatest learning experiences of my life.

I had heard that the key to his success was a willingness to learn from his competitors, big or small. Andrew, I was told, maintained a list of emerging and leading relationship coaches across the Americas and Europe. He would invite the most notable relationship coaches to his home in Lima to collate their different ideas and to profit from their insights and experiences.

When he extended an invitation to me, I thought it might be for the same reason. I decided to accept it since I believed that a single conversation with a distinguished relationship coach could open up diverse paths for me that I had not yet explored. I didn't have anything to lose. It was Andrew who had something to lose, while I had lots to gain.

After we shook hands, Andrew asked if I would mind coming to his home for lunch. "This will allow us an opportunity to open up to each other," he explained. "I'm really looking forward to hearing more about your philosophy about relationships."

"That would be a pleasure. I wouldn't be encroaching on your valuable time or private space?" I replied.

"Mike, if I may call you that, it's an honor to have a person of your eminence grace my abode, and if it makes you feel any better, I only invite select people to my home."

Andrew, renowned as he was, was surprising me with his unassuming nature, amiable temperament, and sense of exclusivity. I was beginning to succumb to his charm, and therein I realized the difference between him and me. Andrew was miles ahead of me, because he had the uncanny ability to make a rival feel larger than life, while he dwarfed his persona in the competitor's presence.

The drive to Andrew's home took twenty minutes. He lived in an exquisite apartment within San Isidro, an upscale area. The elevator opened directly into his living room, which made for a grand spectacle. The room was filled with an ensemble of artifacts, antiques, and paintings that he had collected from the Americas, Europe, Africa, the Middle East, and Asia Pacific. The carpets were Persian, Belgian, and Kashmiri, the sort prized by collectors. The elegantly carved furniture was an amalgam of mahogany, teak, and oak. He told me that every piece of the furniture had a history to it. Some of it had been inherited from his father, and the others bought or restored.

The living room reflected a man of imperial taste and taught me another lesson—behind the successful relationship coach was a globe-trotter with interests in diverse cultures. His sojourns to different parts of the world had enhanced his understanding of human behavior and strengthened his disseminations about the game of life and relationships.

A piano adorned the room as well, and he had acquired it in England several years earlier. He played it each day for an hour, and had mastered many Western classics, thanks to his creative fingers and zest for melodious music. He had wanted to be a pianist by profession, but the dictates of the commercial world had precluded him from doing so. He later chose to make it an avocation to invigorate his spirits and those of clients who felt their lives lacked meaning or were trapped in failing relationships.

"Mike," he said, "the melodic notes from a piano can enchant even a morose heart, and relationships are about bringing smiles to sullen faces."

"I couldn't agree more. Speech is silver and music is golden."

On an antique mahogany side table at one end of the living room, an ivory chessboard was on display. He had acquired it on his first visit to India nine years earlier. The chessboard reminded me of the sagacious advice I had once received from a venerated marketing professor at Northwestern University: "Strategy and the game of chess are analogous. Don't make your first move till you have visualized and calculated your last move."

Andrew asked me if I played chess, and I told him that I did and had learned from a Russian friend.

"The Russians are among the world's best chess players," he said. "I learned chess on my first visit to India, and later polished my moves through frequent sessions with an Indian friend in Chicago. Life is a like a game of chess. Either you make the first move or you are forced to make one."

"What a profound statement. So, do you always make the first move?" I asked as if I was trying to assess his game plan for inviting me over.

"Mike, you're a very intelligent man," he grinned. My moves depend on the people I meet and their cultural ethos. The game of chess has taught me to be patient, flexible, and observant."

His comment revealed his extraordinary ability to connect different interests of life with human characteristics in order to create more meaningful relationships.

It was time I dug deep and asked questions so I could learn more about his approach to enhancing the quality of relationships. After all, he was among the best known relationship gurus, and these privileged moments with him could prove to be the turning point of my career. Over lunch, I asked Andrew what had motivated him to become a relationship coach.

Andrew looked at me with both affection and faith. "Mike, I like you. Your eyes are… tranquil. Something tells me you will surpass me as a relationship coach. Unlike a lot of people, it seems like your heart is in the right place. Trust me, I almost never go wrong in spotting talent, depth, and beauty. I'll tell you my story."

I felt small and embarrassed. Here I was trying to find nefarious motives for him inviting me to Lima, which was alien to my usual trusting disposition. I felt weighed down with remorse, and in a sudden gush of repentance, I said, "Andrew, I need to apologize to you for casting aspersions on your motive for inviting me to Peru. When I first heard from you, I was suspicious as to why a mega relationship coach such as yourself would invite an insignificant relationship adviser like me to your home. I was given to understand that you like to meet your competitors to get ideas to further your own coaching business. And yet I wondered why me, because I am too inconsequential to be your true competitor."

Andrew laughed profusely. "My reputation precedes me. Yes, I like to meet individuals who are making a difference in the lives of many, because I learn from them. I do not see them as competitors, big or small. I see them as collaborators who work with people to bring harmony and deeper meaning to their personal and professional lives. Unlike most people, my competition is only with myself and my goals, not with the sung or unsung heroes. That, my friend, is the cardinal principle of happiness and strong relationships."

Brilliant! I thought. *This man is remarkable.* His profound message reverberated in my head.

"Mike, I was a self-absorbed, rigid, and pompous brat until I met a woman named Dorothy Porter in Chicago seven years ago. Dorothy, in her midthirties, was a senior public relations executive with an advertising agency. I had spent twenty years within the realm of public relations and marketing, and was looking to hire an experienced communications professional for my public-relations agency. A friend recommended Dorothy because she had worked for him as a public-relations associate during the early part of her career. Subsequently, my friend moved out of the public-relations industry, while she continued to hone her skills in advertising and public relations. I met Ms. Porter for the first time at the John Hancock Center in Chicago, to interview her.

She was smart, vivacious, and sparkled with clarity of thought. Her answers to my questions did not seem rehearsed, as she replied with remarkable confidence and self-belief. She was an able communicator, and her choice of words was simply outstanding. Toward the end of the interview, I asked her what the key to success and happiness was. She said immediately, 'Pursue your passion, work with your intuition, learn as a child, and adapt as water.' Her stupefying reply was the turning point of my life. All of a sudden the roles had reversed. While I looked like the interviewer, it was Dorothy who spoke as the interviewer and the communications expert. I had more experience as an entrepreneur and public-relations adviser, I was the hiring manager, but Dorothy would emerge as my change agent. I offered her the job right away and she gladly accepted it.

On my way home, I reflected on Dorothy's statement: 'Pursue your passion, work with your intuition, learn as a child, and adapt as water.' But I was successful, and changing course to pursue my passion was simply not practical. Why did I have to learn or adapt if my business had loyal clients? Why should I act on my instincts if what had got my agency so far had primarily been logic and analytically driven decisions?

Questions and more questions were looming over my mind and disturbing me. I needed answers, so I called Dorothy to see if we could meet up for lunch the next day to go over her precise role and responsibilities. Quite a charade. She agreed, and I promised we would make it quick, because she had loose ends to tie up in her present job before she would quit to join my agency.

The following day was bright and sunny, seeming to herald new beginnings in my life. There was a bounce in my step, a newfound excitement that took me back to the sagacious words of a revered spiritual guru from India I had had the good fortune of meeting. The spiritual master had said, 'Mother Nature does provide a road map to future occurrences. Nature talks and portends your future. You just have to be silent from within to understand what nature has planned for you. When things are meant to go wrong, problems crop up. The otherwise correct decisions are off the mark, well-thought-out plans go haywire, and best efforts yield abortive results. When better times are waiting to happen, positive developments begin to surface. Like a jigsaw puzzle, the positive developments automatically descend from different directions, and time fits the puzzle together to make it one complete happy picture. Learn to study nature and you will get an insight into where life may lead you.' The master's wise words struck a chord with me.

So that sunny day seemed to promise exciting new developments. My body felt newly energized. I was listening to music again after a long time. I had enjoyed my breakfast of poached eggs as never before. The buttered toast was delicious. Hours before our lunch meeting, Dorothy's words were bringing out my true self—an individual who got happiness from all the small acts of life.

I had lost myself to the world of deadlines, stress, materialism, demanding clients, and multi-tasking. I had forgotten the true meaning of growth and happiness, and the importance of intimate rela-tionships. All I knew was schedules, timelines, the Internet, and e-mails. My corporate clients were big companies, and I was aspiring to become one. I had become insular and rigid: if you work for me, you have to do it my way. I was living the life that soci-ety had expected of me. But did anybody really care about me and my success? *No.* I lived with the supe-rior thought that everybody in society was watching each step I took. I was aware of this artificial world, but I had become a part of it because when I was as young as you, I had not met a Dorothy.

Dorothy and I met for lunch at L'Appetito at The Hancock. That place serves a delicious lunch—but it's always difficult to concentrate when both mouth-watering food and an interesting woman are present," he said, and winked.

"I noticed that Dorothy had lovely, lucid eyes. They actually changed colors with the state of her mind! When she delved into intuitive and creative topics, they would turn dark green, and when she spoke about the importance of the rational and logical bent of mind, her eyes would turn light-brown. I gauged her alternating states of mind by asking her a few questions about the artistic and investigative aspects of life, as a precursor to what I really wanted to ask her, the raison d'être of the meeting. I had conveniently forgotten the alibi I had concocted to get her to meet me for lunch, that we were to go over her precise role and responsibilities."

Andrew said their conversation had so affected him, he remembered it word-for-word, and he proceeded to recount it for me.

"Dorothy, before we discuss your responsibilities in further detail, I have to admit that I was fascinated by your response to my question about the key to success and happiness. Could you please talk some more about your philosophy, 'Pursue your passion, work with your intuition, learn as a child, and adapt as water'?"

"Thank you, Andrew," she said, "but I think my response was commonplace."

"On the contrary, it intrigued me no end. Could you please expound on it?"

"If you insist. I'll bore you with pleasure. The first question that every individual needs to ask of him or herself is, 'What is that one profession, vocation, or occupation I would pursue if I did not have to work for money?' That is the key to finding out what you are truly passionate about. If you have the courage to pursue your passion without worrying about monetary concerns or the consequences, then you can attain noteworthy distinction in a lifetime. This journey may be laden in the short run with struggle, failure, and mistakes, but in the long run, happiness, success, and fame will follow. The joys and pleasures of pursuing your passion never end.

After you've figured out your passion and are ready to make the plunge, you have to become one with it, which means rigorous practice toward excellence. This is where you must work with the heart—with your intuition. If you are immersed in what you truly love, an activity you have longed to excel at, a pursuit that will get you closer to prominence, and an endeavor that doesn't feel like work, you'll find happiness. Subsequently, if you have to make tough or important decisions, you only have to stay silent, look within, and you will be guided by an inner voice. The voice of God will steer you through the maze of difficult choices and crossroads.

The next stage is to continue the journey as a child—curious, open-minded, and willing to experiment without fear of failure or rejection. You stay inquisitive, you seek and grow by asking questions. You stay receptive to experiences and occurrences you have not encountered or lived through before. You begin each day as the first day in your journey toward honing your passion. You become a trail-blazer without worrying too much about the end result. Each day you practice or revise, and if you fall down, you get up again. You never say, I know it all or, I have perfected the art. You can only say— to quote a well-known poem— 'I have miles to go before I sleep.'

The last stage in this voyage is to adapt as water. Observe water very closely. In it lies the road to the middle path, the secrets to meaningful rela-tionships and a happy life. Water changes its form as though no shape is certain. This is similar to a man's endeavor to constantly adapt to the condi-tions or circumstances that besiege him, without having any rigid rules. Water floats in and out of different types of vessels and cups, and yet retains its ability to quench thirst. It transforms constantly. Flexible people with water-like traits are the hap-piest in life. Personal and professional camaraderie can be enriched simply by adopting the essence of the water philosophy—remain adaptable."

"Dorothy, I am truly impressed, and I need you to candidly assess where I stand in this four-stage philosophy. Forget that I have hired you—just be honest."

"Are you sure?"

"As certain as I am about hiring you."

"Andrew, it seems to me that deep inside you are not happy with your chosen path. I have to ask you tough questions."

All of a sudden the power equation had changed, Andrew told me. The boss had become the subordinate. The next half hour would redefine his life.

"So, tell me. What is that one passion or path you would pursue if you did not have to work for money?" she asked.

"Dorothy," I said after I'd been quiet for a few minutes, "I've always wanted to own and manage a magazine that focused on common folks and their lives. I commenced my career as a journalist and ten years into the profession, thought of starting my own magazine."

"What prevented you from doing it?"

"Well, I guess—for the same reasons most people don't live their dreams. A risk-averse mindset, the fear of failure or lack of financial security. I was a victim of the play-safe syndrome. Why rock the boat if you have a good job that provides adequate money to pay your bills—and you also get regular bylines as a reporter?"

"As a reporter, did you work zealously?" Dorothy asked.

"I did work long hours, and very hard. As a journalist there is never a dull moment. It's an exciting job. I did enjoy my stint as a senior business reporter. In that sense, I did work feverishly. But did my heart completely lie in my reporting job? No, not really. My heart was always telling me to start a magazine that covered the lives of ordinary people—their emotions, relationships, beliefs…"

"So, in order to help maintain a livelihood, you played it safe and like most people chose to forget your dream. Andrew, that is the difference between successful and great people. You neither chased your passion nor did you put your heart into reporting. You merely worked with your head and followed your interest, but the pursuit of passion is to go after a perceived fantasy and make it a pragmatic possibility. Your path to eminence will begin when you are ready to run after your passion or big dream."

She paused for a minute, looked at me intently, smiled and then posed a question. "Why did you transition from a reporter to a public-relations consultant?"

"It happened. I did not plan it. A friend from the marketing fraternity started his own consultancy company and offered me a job managing media relations and building the brand of the consultancy service. The money was better—it would have helped me save up for my proposed magazine venture. But little did I realize that in the competitive business of marketing and public-relations consultancy, I would lose myself to the demons of profit, deadlines, meetings, budgets, market share, and wily client acquisition tactics.

Over a period of four years, I rose to become a partner and later bought out the company. I had become an entrepreneur with freedom galore. I now wanted to start my own magazine, but the big bucks of the consultancy business and increasing client roster enticed me away from my dream project."

"Time flew by, and the lure of money took you away from your dreams," Dorothy said, smiling again. "But you should be proud of your achievements. You are reasonably well-known, wealthy, and have everything going for you."

"Yes, I do, but what eludes me is the fruition of my cherished dream. That is what makes my life incomplete."

"Why wait? It is never too late. Dreams are attained by those who have the courage to act on their convictions. Remember what I told you, Andrew—pursue your passion, work with your intuition, learn as a child and adapt as water."

Andrew focused on me. "There was something magical about Dorothy's words, which inspired me as never before. A year later, I started a magazine called *People Mantra* that focused on ordinary people, their lives and relationships. Dorothy moved onto *People Mantra* as the editor in chief. Her cogent thoughts helped me reconnect with my lost inner voice."

"I guess *People Mantra* veered you toward your defining moment and directed you to a new path."

"Yes, it did. The magazine connected me to a whole new world of human emotions. I realized how meaningless life had been until that moment. I had made tons of money for my clients and me, but I was poorer because I had not met life and its varied shades.

Mike, *People Mantra* focused on improving the quality of life and relationships. We wanted people to laugh, rethink their career options, enhance communications skills, and suggest ideas to make life a blissful journey. The magazine was an instant winner. The circulation figures, astonishingly, quadrupled within a year of its launch, and as you may know, it became one of America's most talked about magazines. There was never a happier period in my life."

Two

Andrew continued his story.

"*People Mantra* was the culmination of a small man's dream of a national people's magazine that was spurred by Dorothy's philosophy of pursue your passion, work with your intuition, learn as a child, and adapt as water. That became the motto of our magazine. Seldom before had articles and interviews caused an incomparable connection among millions of people. Dorothy's discerning philosophy reverberated in the homes and offices of the magazine's readers. She was delighted she had touched the lives of so many people from all walks of life. And back in our office, those soft words had changed an abrasive, rigid, pompous, and selfish Andrew Smith into a caring, adaptable, and humble individual. She had transformed my life. I was living my dream. That is the power of an exceptional lady's words."

Andrew added, "A woman with beauty and brains is a great combination, but an attractive, smart lady with depth and compassion is ethereal. Dorothy was one such amazing lady. She was a unique woman who could convince you to follow your dreams through her captivating persona and deep eyes. I had never met a woman like her before. You could say anything to her and nothing would surprise her. What you and I may term as ludicrous never astonished her or made her blink. She would always echo the famous words of Oliver Goldsmith, 'Every absurdity has a champion to defend it,' and relate that with people and happiness."

She said, "Happiness is synonymous with the kind of people you associate with. The bibliophile finds meaning in books, the wise in sagacious company, the socialite in material trappings, the spiritual seeker in profundity, the money lender in money, and the actor in acting. Each person has different ways of seeking happiness. This must be understood to manage complex human relationships better.

Slowly and surely, I fell in love with Dorothy. She was an apparition of delight whose inner beauty overshadowed everything around her. She was not what most people would think of as gorgeous, yet she was a woman any discriminating man would yearn for."

"What made her so special?" I asked.

"Well… a conventionally beautiful woman

appeals to most the moment she enters a room. Stunning women can sweep men off their feet. Outward beauty has a possessing power, although it is short-lived. Dorothy had staying power. She was not the kind of woman most would notice instantly, but if you spent time with her, she would grow on you to the point that you could not imagine a day without her."

"Staying power versus fleeting power. Very interesting," I said.

"Dorothy made people fall in love with her because of her magnetic aura, soft understated style of communications, remarkable choice of words, strength of character and a tender touch that could assuage concern or anguish. A cologne's fragrance lingers only for a few hours, but she was a breath of fresh air that would carry your senses to a new world."

"That is a lovely portrayal of a woman of substance. But to err is human?" I asked.

"Dorothy was not infallible or above mistakes. She did have her share of omissions, but was secure enough to promptly accept them. She felt that mistakes honed her work and were accurate indicators of where she stood in pursuit of true excellence."

"That is a remarkably uncommon trait. Surely that would have made her an incredible editor and colleague?"

"Of course. And yet, as is with most outstanding professionals, she made a faux pas. Caroline Gerber, a senior and experienced reporter on the magazine's staff, had filed a major story about different ethnicities in the US, and what common purpose connected these people to make an association. Dorothy always liked what Caroline wrote for *People Mantra,* but this time around she wanted Caroline to rewrite some parts of the story—she felt it lacked the emotional punch to strike a chord with the readers. Caroline disagreed. She tried to convince Dorothy that the content of the article was inspiring enough to resonate with the readers. Dorothy was not persuaded.

Caroline suggested the story be forwarded to me for my views, and if I felt a change was required, she would gladly do so. Caroline was very passionate about her work, and had a great sense of what went into putting out exceptional articles. She had more reporting experience than Dorothy and me, and was among the most admired reporters in Chicago. Caroline was open to edits to her stories, but not dramatic rewrites, while Dorothy thought that rewrites were a cogent way to make a story more effective. I was asked to make a judgment call.

I read Caroline's story and thought it was splendid. The article was moving and inspirational and I was sure it would resonate with the readers. Dorothy, used to working on hunches, did not change her opinion about Caroline's piece, but went with the flow because of me, and the article was published without any changes.

Caroline was wrong, and so was I. Unlike her earlier stories, this piece did not get the accolades she was used to, and it bruised her ego. It had been over a decade since an article she'd written got an unenthusiastic response. She had vowed to herself then that it would never happen again. Regrettably, a decade later, it did.

She decided to pass the buck to Dorothy for the lukewarm response to her story. After all, what went into print was the overall responsibility of the editor in chief. The rumor mills started doing the rounds. The entire staff thought it was Dorothy's editorial oversight that had led to Caroline's mediocre story and negative feedback.

Dorothy summoned Caroline—but not to reproach her. Instead, she wanted to comfort Caroline and reiterate that she was among the best reporters in the country. Indeed, *People Mantra* was fortunate to have her on board. Caroline took Dorothy's words otherwise and thought Dorothy was having a dig at her story.

Caroline told her she had gotten her job because of me and not because of her abilities. An enraged Caroline then walked out of Dorothy's office. Dorothy was hurt but decided it was a very small matter to lose sleep over."

"Andrew, I don't understand. Why do you say Dorothy committed a faux pas?"

"Mike, the contest between an accomplished

secure individual and a successful arrogant person exists only in the mind of the latter. For the egotistical, defeat is unacceptable, and external victories are a way of feeling secure. For the accomplished secure, it does not matter because all battles are waged within the self and not outside. Dorothy never competed with anybody but herself, while Caroline saw every woman as a competitor. She detested losing to another woman. And even though Caroline had more reporting and editorial experience, Dorothy was Caroline's supervisor.

Caroline had joined *People Mantra* because she wanted to work for a new and dynamic media company. Little did she realize that she would have to report to Dorothy. She resented this relationship. She thought that her work would overshadow Dorothy's profile, leaving her envious, and Dorothy might quit. But Dorothy was as sensitive as a flower and always praised Caroline's contribution to *People Mantra*.

The day Caroline was invited to interview with Dorothy, a dear friend of Dorothy passed away. In her absence, I met Caroline. I was aware of her reporting competence, but ambivalent about her comfort levels working for Dorothy. I expressed that to Dorothy later in the day, but she insisted that we hire her because of her experience and reporting skills. I was not convinced but went with Dorothy's judgment.

Sometimes it is better to let sleeping dogs lie. At the

end of the alleged editorial oversight episode, Dorothy's attempt to comfort Caroline about her reporting abilities ignited her fragile ego. Caroline resigned from *People Mantra* and moved to our biggest competitor, but not without poaching three key senior reporters who moved with her to our archrivals. While *People Mantra* lost valuable experience, Caroline was indeed over the moon."

"Where is Dorothy now?" I asked.

"Her vision and charisma made the magazine an interesting read and a great reference point for people from all sections of society. She and I had become very close friends. But best of friends do part and all good things do end—perhaps a momentary pause for life to take another direction.

Dorothy moved to Peru three and a half years ago. For the first six months we were in touch, but for some inexplicable reason she stopped responding to my e-mails three years ago. I tried calling her, to no avail. Since then I have lost touch with her."

"Andrew don't you long to meet her, talk to her, and have her presence around you? Don't you feel powerless – a celebrated relationship coach as you who the world follows and looks up to, could not attract an incomparable woman with his admiration and love?" I asked curiously.

"The enrapturing touch of a woman is gratifying to the senses. But true love goes beyond carnal desire to continually feeling an omnipotent force of togetherness. I feel she is always with me."

Andrew paused for a moment and continued, "I may have spent a short period of time with Dorothy, but I feel I have known her for ages. Her persona consummates my mind, body, and spirit in a way that I see her, talk to her, and smile at her. That is the depth of my love and admiration for her. It is sheer bliss."

"How did you transition from *People Mantra* to a relationship coach?" I asked.

"The magazine taught me a great lesson that irrespective of color, creed, ethnicity, or community, human emotions and needs are similar universally. The difference lies in how individuals manage their moments of joy and despair. Readers in large numbers would continually write to me asking for relationship advice within their personal and professional realm. This was another opportunity to enrich people's lives, and I instinctively decided to turn into a relationship coach. Subsequently, I sold *People Mantra* to the employees of the magazine and moved onto my new role. It has been a journey of ceaseless growth. When you are supposed to be the relationship expert, you realize how important it is to look for happiness in the small things of life. All of a sudden you are blessed with the power to influence the lives of many, and that brings with it a huge responsibility of being able to connect with disparate people and their emotions.

The seeds of my reincarnation as a relationship coach were sown by Dorothy. She would always say, 'Live as if today is your last day on this planet and remember to wear this on your sleeve each day. You will then become the best friend, the favorite supervisor, the unrivaled sweetheart, the wisest adviser, and the greatest listener.'

Good beginnings make good endings. The interview with Dorothy at the John Hancock Center was timeless – never before would an interviewer's destiny be shaped by the golden words of an interviewee."

"Dorothy must be a very fascinating woman," I said.

"Yes, she is, and I'm glad I shared some of the most private moments of my life with you, including Dorothy's precious philosophy," Andrew said, lowering his voice.

"I am truly blessed. Thank you very much."

"Mike, I've read about you. But what induced me to invite you to Lima was not only because your career mirrors mine, but also for the reason that you have played varied roles in life—journalist, writer, consultant, and now a relationship coach for young folks. My gut told me there is something quite unique about you. My urge to pass on the treasured philosophy is critical. I am suffering from cancer. I will die soon."

"What! I am so sorry." I was taken aback and could not believe what I had just heard. My eyes and words were not in synchrony. I did not know what more to say to Andrew, except, "How is it that you seem so unflappable?"

"Thanks to Dorothy, I live life each day as if it is my last date with existence. Death is inevitable, so I enjoy the remaining opportunity to regale myself with many fond and precious memories that I have shared with Dorothy. Can anything be more delightful?"

To see a man dying of a dreaded disease without an iota of pain or fear in his eyes… I was speechless with admiration.

"The successor to Dorothy's invaluable gems has to be creative, sharp-witted, profound, and comparatively much younger than me—but more importantly, I am looking for somebody who has experienced a wide variety of careers, including success and failure, and yet has the nerve to make it very big. You are a fitting candidate. You know now why I opened up my heart to you. In you I see the inheritor to a philosophy that could bring happiness into the lives of the young and their relationships. After all, it is the youth who influence the destiny of a nation. But something tells me that I still have a story to hear—your story and what made you a relationship coach?" Andrew said adorning his curiosity cap. He had deflected the possibility of any further discussion of his cancer by throwing in a question at me.

"I am honored and touched to know that you consider me worthy enough to inherit the lessons imparted by Dorothy. It would be my privilege to carry the baton of that wise philosophy to those who need it," I said as I extended my hand to thank Andrew. I wanted to hug him, but if I did, I would cry. A dying man does not need tears; he needs happy faces and smiles.

"The memoirs of my life," I continued, "would read as an individual who tried his hands at different things not because he planned it that way, it just happened. Life constantly threw trials and opportunities my way. Trials and opportunities are two sides of the same coin - I gleefully accepted them," I replied with a pensive look.

"My journey from a student to a relationship coach taught me that life is meant to explore, take risks and pursue your true calling to discover yourself. However, later I found out that self-discovery was not what I was content with. Getting more out of life than a breakthrough was the road I wanted to tread in order to become big and famous.

I commenced my career as a business reporter, and after a few years of tight deadlines and bylines, started to feel bored and restless. Around the same time, I was offered an external communications job by a management consultancy company in Chicago.

I was asked to harness the brand of the consultancy firm through publicity and media management. My strong writing skills and set of contacts within the media fraternity got the consultancy a lot of coverage and spotlight in the prominent print and electronic media companies in the country. I thought I did a great job."

"No strange coincidence that you and I were both business reporters who transitioned into a public relations job within the consultancy business," Andrew interjected.

"Absolutely. Not to forget we are both from Chicago," I quipped.

"Over the next six years," I went on more seriously, "I also learned the nuances of corporate strategy from my mentor, David Cooney, who initiated me into the business side of the consultancy company. Subsequently, I was made the director responsible for recommending business strategies to big institutional clients, with a team of fifteen consultants, associates, and research professionals assisting me. I was traveling three weeks a month, living out of suitcases and managing high-profile clients. I became a very important man within the consulting business, but deep inside I was dissatisfied because I had no time to write. I had always been a good writer, but lacked the self-confidence to become a full-time writer because I had never been to a writing school. I had donned the role of a reporter because

I confused my passion for writing with a career in journalism, only to realize later that journalism and a craze for writing is not exactly the same thing.

Some months later, a friend introduced me to the wise words of the Chinese philosopher Confucius: Choose a job you love, and you will never have to work a day in your life. Those words left an indelible impression on my mind. I decided to take the plunge and resigned from the consultancy job to become a full-time freelance writer.

Given my experiences, I could write on several topics. This made my decision easier. My writing encompassed wide-ranging themes as business, entrepreneurship, marketing, public relations, leadership and human resources, and I even wrote short stories. Major print publications carried my articles. My published words got me recognition and decent money, but not the kind of adulation I thought I was worthy of. A sense of having made it was missing, because fame did come but never stayed long enough. Perhaps I had to redefine my writing career and conjure something spectacular for the world to remember me by, so I thought of becoming an author. That is, someone who writes books. The time had come to jump of the cliff," I laughed abashedly and in reciprocation opened my heart to a new friend and mentor who had already welcomed me as his protégé.

"The journey from being a writer to an author

was interesting. I had to fall in love all over again, but this time around with lots of words and sentences. Romancing words is an immersion into a journey of self-expression. I rediscovered myself as I wrote about the essence of life and its connection to all forms of existence—relationships.

As I wrote, I realized that as a writer all I had written ever about was centered on people, their attainments, emotions, behavior, skill sets, and how these were aligned with various disciplines and management functions."

"Relationships are complicated and invariably involve mind games. So what is the title of your book and what makes it different?" Andrew asked.

"*Relationships—24/7*," I replied.

"That is a great title. What is the essence of the book?" Andrew asked.

"Thank you. My book focuses on going back to the basics of a sound relationship—compassionate communication and acceptance. Meaningful relationships require compassionate communication and a high level of acceptance to thrive.

The book did pretty well, although it conspicuously resounded with younger people who were struggling in their personal or professional lives. As an author, I was able to ameliorate their knotty relationship dilemmas. Smiling faces, increasing thank-you e-mails and phone calls provided tremendous personal satisfaction, but I had still not made it large or created a big difference. For that to happen, I would have to focus and work closely with a sizeable global population of young people. It was time to turn into a relationship coach for the young. At the back of my mind, a fervent desire had taken root—I have to touch more young lives than anyone has ever done before so that history will remember me as an individual whose solutions provided hope and cheer to the younger generation universally."

"So you became a relationship coach for the young because you wanted to be remembered by history and play a crucial role in redefining the lives of the young?" Andrew asked with a wry smile on his face.

"To stand out in history, you have to take on new paths and charter your own course. And if you become famous by means of noble intentions, you can ignite a fire that can brighten the lives of many people. All my inadvertent career moves had a common connection—people and relationships. I have an inkling that it is this blend of people and relationships that will take me to the path of eminence."

"And what makes you think you have missed it so far?"

"I believe a man cannot become a luminary without the presence of an extraordinary woman in his life. I did not have a Dorothy to help me make it big."

"I agree. I became an internationally recognized

coach because of Dorothy. She was the reason behind my confidence and larger purpose to life. Every time I met with her, I felt I could take on the world."

"She was also behind the spectacular growth of your magazine. I really hope a special woman's Midas touch will make my published voice or book a best seller too," I said.

"Mike, just so you know, I've read your book. I liked it. You have a compassion index that is out of the ordinary, and perhaps best expressed through a book. Make sure you write a book each year. You will leave a rich legacy that will serve and strengthen generations to come. Go forth and make history," Andrew said warmly.

His commendation was inspiring and touching, enough to move me to tears.

The lunch at Andrew's apartment was one of the best meals of my life. Those few hours with him had taught me more about life than I had learned in school, college, university, or my varied career paths. Everything happens for a reason, and my lunch with Andrew was integral to the Almighty's master plan, which had brought me on an unusual trip to Peru, thousands of miles away from my home.

A spiritual master in India had said, "Nature portends your future. God gifts the skills of prognostication to humans for understanding future occurrences. You just have to be internally placid to understand his plan for you." Could this mean that my early morning dream would come true? A lady dressed in white would walk me to the beautiful Pacific Ocean and whisper, "The ethereal ocean will now bring a wave of graces your way. Keep your inner door open to receive the special graces and discover your true destiny."

Only time had an answer… and I was curious.

Three

I caught a taxi to return to the Del Pilar Miraflores Hotel and headed back to my room for a small nap. But I could not sleep. I was like a cat on a hot tin roof, edgy and angst ridden. Andrew's captivating portrayal of Dorothy had stirred my imagination. Was there a way to find out where she lived in Peru? We live in a wired world. I could ascertain her whereabouts via the Internet and social media, I told myself.

I jumped from the bed and got my tablet to go online. There was a spring to my step. I felt the entire world's energy was within one person—me. Google and LinkedIn suddenly had a new meaning in my life. My heart was pounding with nervous excitement, for the Internet has an amazing search and interactive capacity to bring missing or disengaged people together.

Within a minute, I was staring at the Google

home page. I typed *Dorothy Porter*, and it threw up several hundred names and possibilities, including numerous posts about a famous Australian poet named Dorothy Porter. The effort to rummage around these proved futile. I refined the search and typed *Dorothy Porter in Latin America,* but to my disappointment found no information. I went back to *Dorothy Porter* and improvised it by trying other locations, such as Lima, Peru; Chicago; and the US. I was delighted as I got lots of links with information about her as a communications professional with Andrew's PR agency and editor at *People Mantra.* I perused each of these links, but all I found was old contact information.

For the next four hours, all my search attempts to find any current contact details were in vain. All possible permutations and combinations on various search engines did not lead me to *the* Dorothy Porter, Andrew had known. Exultation was supplanted by dejection. It dawned on me then that Andrew must have used all possible search engines and social networking sites to find Dorothy in Peru. I laughed at my foolishness and belated realization. It was 8:30 p.m. Time to take a break, head for the shower, and savor a glass of the exquisite pisco sour. Subsequently, I had space in my stomach for only a light dinner. I called it a day at ten.

The next morning, I decided to pay a visit to Larcomar, an outdoor mall considered the premier tourism and entertainment center in Lima. I was told that apart from being the most fashionable shopping center, it provided the best view of Miraflores Bay.

Larcomar has more than eighty stores with everything from souvenirs to electronics, including incredible restaurants. It was a lovely sight to behold. And indeed I surveyed Larcomar with disbelief. I'd had no idea that the ocean that appeared in my dream would welcome me at Larcomar. Hanging off a cliff above the Pacific Ocean is… Larcomar. Was this the setting where I would meet the attractive woman from my dream? Would this ocean bring a wave of graces my way? I could not believe my eyes, even as I witnessed a breathtaking view of the ocean from both outside and inside the stores.

The Pacific Ocean was as clear as crystal, as pure as winter snow, and as beautiful as the rainbow—and I was as speechless as a stone. That gigantic ocean seemed to have a large heart that would embrace all who viewed its magnificence. Its waves were calm, and the balmy breeze gently ruffled my hair. A picturesque view of the endless deep blue ocean filled my heart with the sound of music and a serene stillness I had not experienced before. It felt as if I was meditating with open eyes.

Every so often, the logical corollary of a tranquil mind is high spirits. You know how uplifted you feel at times, such as when you think you are in love with the world and everything in it, when your heart seems full to bursting. I was in an exalted state of mind, bubbling with buoyant energy and oblivious to the visitors around me who had dropped in for an outing at Larcomar.

"Excuse me, do you mind telling me the time?" a tourist asked, waking me from my meditative frame of mind.

It was 12 p.m., and after experiencing such empyreal bliss, it was the appropriate hour to enjoy a pisco sour with the scenic surroundings. I ambled toward La Dama Juana, one of the finest restaurants at Larcomar.

"Señor, a glass of pisco sour for you," the waiter said.

"*Gracias,*" I replied, which was about the extent of my limited Spanish.

As I relished my first sip of the drink, I heard a lovely voice say, "George, test your relationship before you tie the knot." The mesmerizing voice came from behind. I turned around and saw an attractive woman in animated conversation with a man in a suit, his back to me. I could not help but eavesdrop on the conversation. The subject was relationships, and I was in the business of relationships.

"But that would mean casting aspersions on the character of my girlfriend," George answered. "Are you telling me that my sweetheart has to pass a character test to be eligible to marry me?"

"Let me make this simple for you. People who

fall in love and marry only for material gain are the most unfortunate individuals. Marry for love and not for money seems old-fashioned, but it provides eternal happiness. Material abundance devoid of love and trust can provide a house, but not a home. Billions of dollars in wealth, but not even a thousand dollars of happiness." the comely lady responded.

"I couldn't agree with you more, but Sarah loves me and not my wealth," George replied.

"And how sure are you about that?"

"I am without a job and she is still seeing me, although we do spend less time with each other these days."

"And why is that?"

"Because she has been saddled with work," George answered.

"Has this happened before?"

"No, just recently."

"And have you asked her what has led to the sudden increase in her workload?"

"I did, and she mentioned demanding clients and their pressing deadlines. I understand because I've worked in the advertising business too."

"Did her work hours increase around the same time as you got laid off?"

"Yes. But that could be sheer coincidence," George said.

"Sure. But I have seen enough coincidences like

your situation to know what Sarah may be thinking. She is in a conundrum."

"Conundrum? You mean she is of two minds?" George asked.

"Yes. I have had far too many clients and friends in similar situations, and I can tell you that when adversity strikes, the closest betray while the farthest save the day. Strength of character is an important attribute, which should be gauged before a person falls in love. Love based merely on the allure of material success invariably ends up in a disaster for one of the individuals in the relationship," the woman said wisely.

"I am not quite convinced with your concept of 'test your beloved' before embarking on a journey of marital bliss."

"Well, I can understand your predicament because what I suggest sounds absurd, at least when you hear it for the first time. However, I urge you to consider it."

"Have any of your clients or friends put their beloved to a test?" George asked.

"Nobody did so without resistance, but those who followed my suggestion were spared the ignominy of a bad relationship or failed marriage."

As I overheard the conversation, I could not help but agree with the blond woman's theory—test your beloved before you make any future plans. My experience as a relationship adviser had been similar. I had witnessed a number of clients go through miserable relationships only because, prior to making a final commitment, they did not test the strength of their beloved's character.

I was reminded of Chris Paddington, a seasoned marketing professional in Chicago. Chris had been my client a year earlier. He was inquisitive, well-read, and an interesting conversationalist. Chris was dating Samantha, and they seemed to be deeply in love—until I suggested he feign adversity to see if his love was true and could stand the test of time.

Chris rejected my suggestion as a "ludicrous proposition," only to come back a few days later to accept my challenge. He loved challenges and proving people wrong. What better way to send out a message that he had caught a reasonably well-known relationship coach wide off the mark? He agreed to put Samantha to the test. He lied to her that he had lost his job, when in fact he had been elevated to the marketing director's post at his company. Within the first week of his camouflaged test, he observed that Samantha started evading him and would only take his calls once a day. She was an incurable romantic and would always speak with Chris at least three times a day before.

The transition from three conversations a day to one a day got Chris thinking. He had begun to smell a rat. However, he decided to adopt a wait-and-see approach. A week became a month, and the once-a-day casual cell-phone talks changed to formal three-times-a-week conversations. As the number and duration of calls decreased, he decided it was time for some action.

One fine morning, out of the blue, Chris accosted Samantha outside her office.

She immediately explained her lack of support. "Honey," she said, "I am so sorry for not being around during your darkest hour. The layoff must be very tough on you. But I have been inundated with tight client deadlines and multiple projects."

As luck would have it, that evening Chris saw Samantha with her friends at a restaurant. It was only 5:30 p.m., and he wondered how she could be at a restaurant at that time when all he'd heard on the phone over the past month was that she kept having to work late because she had so much going on. He shook his head in disbelief and disgust. He immediately called her office. Posing as one of her clients, he was able to find out her work schedule for the past week. To his utter surprise, he learned that Samantha had never stayed late that week. He was hurt and had tears in his eyes. His implicit trust in Samantha had been shattered. Apparently, she had loved him only because of his awesome job, which she believed would ensure she would enjoy all luxuries she had planned for her life. Chris left the restaurant with a broken heart.

The next morning, once again he caught

Samantha unawares outside her office and demanded an explanation for her strange behavior over the past month. He knew it was not the right time or place to talk, but he believed in the power of surprise. What was true often came out in the open when a person was faced with something unexpected.

Samantha was at first reluctant to talk, but when Chris cajoled her, she bluntly said, "Chris, you've lost your job and are still unemployed. I don't associate with losers. Love can't buy the comforts of life. I'm sorry, but I do not see a future with you. It's best we move on."

Chris was heartbroken but politely walked away, as he saw no point in convincing a materialistic Samantha that no two days in life are the same.

To his credit, he assimilated the painful truth, and an hour later called her to reveal the truth. He startled her with the test-your-beloved theory that he had been acting on for the past month. Obviously stunned, Samantha apologized and promised unconditional love. But he was wiser. Samantha could only care for him when he was successful; if he were to falter, she would be the first person to dump him. Though a small test of true love, the toughest challenge of his life had saved him from an empty marriage. His love was not true to him; she was true to wealth.

Chris told me later, "Mike, this was a challenge I

thought I would win hands down. I wanted to prove you wrong. For the first time in my life, I am glad I lost a challenge. Never before has a lost contest called for a celebration."

*

"Señor, would you like another pisco sour?" the waiter asked, bringing me back to the present from my journey down memory lane. From Lima to Chicago, my mind had wandered into the past and within a few minutes traversed the distance between cities in two different countries. The mind, I thought, was faster than the wind and could travel around the world without a fee.

I had read somewhere that in ancient India, revered saints would exclaim, "He who conquers the wandering mind can rule the world." I realized then that an important aspect of successful relationship management was to listen to another person with the mind, body, and spirit all focused on that person, so that the mind didn't feel the need to wander.

It was time I focused on the present and continue to listen in on the conversation between the woman and George. I subtly and slowly moved my chair a few inches closer so that I could catch every word. They were discussing one of my favorite topics—love and economics.

"Love that revolves around money and glamour cannot thrive at any cost," the woman was saying.

"But is it realistic to expect love not to have any material expectations?" George asked.

"George, a strong bond and captivating fondness are beyond financial calculations. The strength of true love can make even the smallest home feel like a mansion."

"But you need money to pay bills and satiate your desires."

"Sure you need adequate money to take care of your needs, and I'm not suggesting you shouldn't earn money. But falling in love for money and dumping a person while he's going through a bad phase can only be termed as the love of economics."

"I agree with the essence of your statement, but everybody has the freedom to make a choice. Love over money or money over love."

"Sure they do. In comparison, money is easy to make while genuine love is hard to find. Those who choose money over love may get very rich in the short run, but they will find themselves alone and lonely in the long-term. The lure of the lucre beguiles and the glitter of materialism deceives."

"But why can't love and money go together?"

"Money and love can go together provided it starts with love. Money is important and required to buy food, clothes, a house, a car, and all the objects that provide transient pleasure, but it cannot provide eternal happiness. That role belongs to love. Why do you think many successful men have attributed their accomplishments to a woman? Because true love is rare and inspired them to make a difference or reach higher."

"True love is a lot of hard work," George said.

"I'm not saying love is just about making vows or romance. Love is about emerging as the alter ego of the suitor. A happy relationship means working on adopting the same interests, condoning faults, accepting quirks or a different temperament, providing room to experiment, space to evolve, and more importantly, honing the ability to have long conversations. With age, conversation skills become as imperative as any other aspect of a fulfilling relationship.

George, too many times people get into a relationship or marriage because of the wrong reasons, only to regret it later. And if you want to make an appropriate or good choice, I suggest you test your girlfriend Sarah, particularly when you're presently unemployed. The rest is up to you."

"Dorothy, I'm confused. My heart disagrees with you, but my head wishes to follow your advice."

Dorothy. Had I heard the name Dorothy? Was the blond woman the extraordinary Dorothy, Andrew had known? Was I only a few feet away from *People Mantra*'s famed editor in chief? Could destiny spring such a big surprise in Lima?

My heart was pounding. I was nervous with excitement. I had to make sure I met her to ascertain if she was Andrew's Dorothy. But would she talk to me if I mentioned Andrew? Was it appropriate to intrude on an important conversation between Dorothy and George? After all, I was a stranger to both.

I had to remind myself that great achievements cannot be attained without boldness or self-assurance. I plucked up my courage, abandoned my pisco sour, got up from my table, and walked toward Dorothy and George. Never before in my life had I felt the urge to meet a stranger so strongly.

"Excuse me," I said to them both. "My apologies for encroaching on your time and privacy." I turned to the woman. "May I ask you if you're Dorothy Porter of *People Mantra* fame?"

"And why would you want to meet Dorothy Porter?" she asked.

"I was an avid reader of *People Mantra* and loved her editorials. Her words touched my life in different ways."

"Thank you. Well, that was a long time ago. I'm no longer a part of the media industry. I am just a facilitator of relationships and I'm not sure how can I help you."

Her admission and introduction did not have any traces of self-importance. I could neither hide my joy nor could I believe that less than a day after I had spent hours online trying to find her, she had appeared before me. Miracles do happen. Certain things are beyond the World Wide Web and its search capacity.

"Let me offer my sincere apologies to both of you," I said. "I confess that I overheard some of your conversation because it involved my profession, which is the business of relationships. Dorothy, your thoughts have always intrigued me. You have no idea how much I've wanted to meet you. When I heard your name, I could not stop myself," I finished with a beaming smile. I was in seventh heaven.

"You should be sorry for eavesdropping on our conversation," George said with disgust. "Personal matters are private and off the record. However, I can well understand how eager you must have been to meet Dorothy. She is indeed an amazing person." His facial expression changed, revealing his respect for Dorothy.

"I am very sorry, George," I said. "Nevertheless, I assure you that your personal matter will always remain confidential. My name is Michael Elliott, and I am a relationship coach for young people, based out of Chicago." I presented both of them with my business card.

"Dorothy, I would really like to meet you at your convenience," I went on, "and discuss the world of relationships. I promise you it will be short. You can decide the time and date."

Dorothy closed her eyes, seeming to ponder my request, and almost a minute later replied,

"Michael, I am enthused by the passion and energy you exude. I'm not sure if I can provide you anything as meaningful as you believe, but if you insist, we can meet tomorrow."

"I'm getting greedy. Can we please meet for lunch? You name the place," I said. I was being cheeky, but I knew my persistence would pay off.

"I like your confidence. Will 12:30 work for you?"

"That would be perfect."

"Where are you staying?" she asked.

"At the Del Pilar Miraflores Hotel," I replied.

"In that case, it may be a good idea to have lunch at a restaurant in Miraflores."

"Since I am new to Lima, I will go along with your recommendation."

"Do you like Italian food?" Dorothy asked.

"Yes, I do."

"Then let us meet at Donatello Restaurant. It is located on Avenida José Pardo 1010 in Miraflores."

"That would be wonderful. I look forward to our meeting tomorrow. Thank you, and once again my heartfelt apologies for intruding on your discussion."

The impossible had happened. What Andrew was searching for, I had found. Dorothy Porter did not know I had met Andrew. I thought it best to keep that little secret to myself and bring it up with Dorothy at an appropriate time.

I did not know why Dorothy had stopped

responding to Andrew. I had to respect her reasons for doing so, but I also had to find out why. I owed that to the dying Andrew.

Just as I bid the Pacific Ocean adieu for now and was leaving Larcomar to head back to the hotel, an inexplicable thought popped into my mind. Could Dorothy be the attractive woman who had appeared in my uncharacteristic dream and led me to the Pacific Ocean?

My trip to Lima was beginning to unravel a new chapter in my life.

FOUR

In eager anticipation of my tryst with Dorothy, which was barely twelve hours away as I lay awake in my hotel bed, I could not help but think of our imminent conversation, the questions I would ask to make it a meaningful rendezvous, and how to slowly but surely lead to the reason for her disengaging with Andrew. I was keen to have a perfect date with Dorothy and not leave anything to chance. So I rehearsed my questions and visualized us engaged in deep conversation well into the early hours of the morning, before my drowsy eyes coerced me to sleep.

The alarm on my phone buzzed and bullied me to wake up at 8 a.m. The first thought that ignited my groggy self was my indispensable energy propeller—food. A shower later, I treated my craving stomach to a sumptuous breakfast at Van Gogh restaurant, which also offered a breathtaking view of the Park of Miraflores. For me, happiness begins with a cup of tea, and on a morning as special as "Dorothy's day," this cup of tea seemed as soothing as the first breath of spring. The delightful Friday morning breakfast, consisting of toast, eggs, fruits, and juice, appeared as divine as the laughter of a baby.

An hour later I sauntered to the nearby Starbucks for a classic chai tea latte as I continued to think about possible reasons for Dorothy's and Andrew's estrangement. Had Dorothy discovered the depth of Andrew's love and admiration for her? Had their apparently platonic relationship, in a moment of weakness, turn amorous? Had Dorothy had a boyfriend who didn't approve of Andrew and their extraordinary friendship? Had Andrew hurt Dorothy? Surely there was a cogent reason for the silence.

I arrived at the Donatello restaurant well ahead of the appointed time, perhaps because I was new to Lima, knew very little Spanish, and did not want Dorothy to show up before me. The golden rule of showing up for a date or a meeting before the lady arrives is important and must be adhered to irrespective of culture or country. The quiet and cozy ambiance of the restaurant was precisely what I had been hoping for to set the tone for a memorable luncheon.

Waiting for a special lady can be quite a test.

The minutes appear as hours and patience gives way to edginess. And yet a moment comes when the wait is over and the heart starts to pound rapidly, and I smiled with relief when Dorothy appeared.

"Thank you for agreeing to meet me at such a short notice," I said.

"The pleasure is entirely mine," she answered. "I must confess, your intrusion yesterday into George's and my conversation at La Dama Juana was quite bold of you, and you know that it is the bold who go far in life," she added.

"Thank you. Well, I take my chances, and if I had missed out on a conversation with you, that would have been a huge loss."

"So what brings you to Lima?" Dorothy asked.

"I was invited to Lima to speak with young people about relationships."

"Wonderful. So did you make an impression with your audience?"

"Sometimes life gives you more than you deserve. This trip is alluding to epochal changes in my life. How else can I explain this unexpected tryst? Whether it is preordained, sheer coincidence, or luck that I inadvertently found Dorothy Porter in a restaurant by the Pacific Ocean in Lima, one thing is for sure. Your presence here is a blessing that will transform my life for the better," I replied.

Given her unassuming disposition, Dorothy clearly felt embarrassed by my praise. She adroitly diverted the compliment and said, "I am hungry. Do you mind if we order food and continue our conversation after?"

"As you please, as long as you recommend what I should order, given that this is my first visit to Donatello," I said, passing over the menu to her.

"Well, if you enjoy spaghetti, I would suggest Suprema de Pollo con Spaghetti a la Sorrentina."

"Couldn't have asked for anything better," I replied as I perused the menu to check if they served pisco sour.

"I presume you would like a Donatello Sour to accompany the spaghetti," Dorothy remarked as if she had read my mind. At my surprised glance, she added, "You did seem to savor pisco sour at Larcomar yesterday."

"Sharp-eyed. That is impressive."

"Observation enhances the quality of a conversation. I am sure as the author of *Relationships—24/7*, you would know that better than I," a smiling Dorothy replied.

"You surprise me in more ways than I expected. How do you know about my book?"

"The online world hides no one and reveals all," she said. She gestured to a waitress and placed the lunch order.

I chuckled. "Dorothy, your recent and private life is certainly off limits for the Internet."

"I treat my personal life as classified information. I believe silence is golden and privacy is platinum."

"Well said. Enigma creates an irresistible pull, which perhaps explains why you are such an intriguing lady."

"Thank you. I do hope that you remember why we are here. You wanted to discuss the world of relationships with me." Once again her modesty reminded me not to digress from the purpose of our lunch meeting.

"I am a successful relationship coach, and yet I have not received the kind of recognition I believe I am worthy of," I remarked candidly.

"So you are in this to be famous?" Dorothy asked.

"I can live with little material pleasures, but I cannot live life devoid of eminence," I replied.

"Why do you think fame has eluded you?"

"I would attribute it to the absence of an *extraordinary* woman in my life."

"So you believe that it requires an exceptional woman to take you from success to prominence? Is this based on sixth sense, contemplation, or reason?"

"A recurring dream," I said.

"Is it an *aspiration* dream or a *sleep* dream?" Dorothy asked.

"An uncharacteristic early-morning dream where a lady dressed in white leads me to the majestic Pacific Ocean and whispers in my ear, 'The ethereal ocean will now bring a wave of graces your way.

Keep your inner door open to receive the special graces and discover your true destiny.' This dream alludes to absence of an extraordinary woman in my life who can show the way to illustriousness."

"Fascinating and unusual. You are destined to meet an exceptional woman soon."

Just then I noticed that Dorothy was dressed in a white T-shirt, and the calm expression on her face resembled the serenity of the attractive woman in my morning dream.

Mysterious are the ways of destiny. A beauty of providence is how the game of preordained occurrences unravels in the most unexpected locations and situations.

"I may be speaking out of turn," I said, "yet I do so with the strong intuitive sense that you are the extraordinary woman my dream alluded to."

Dorothy went on a spree of roaring laughter, thunderous enough to catch the attention of all the guests and staff in the restaurant. A few seconds later, an angelic smile and a deep gaze supplanted the mirth. Her eyes were mystical and beautiful, while my eyes said it all—I was awestruck. Dorothy knew she had me all wrapped up.

"Michael, I can't imagine being the woman who appears in a stranger's dream."

"I have never felt this strongly. You have to trust me. It is no strange coincidence that we met at Larcomar, which is right by the Pacific Ocean. It is no twist of fate that you are dressed in white. It is not a fluke that you are a facilitator of relationships and I am a relationship coach for young people. This rendezvous is preordained. You are destined to lead me to my true place." Looking directly at her, I fervently pleaded my case.

Dorothy was all ears. The beatific disposition came through a few minutes later as she acquiesced to my request.

"Michael, have you ever been in love?" she asked.

"Yes."

"Have you ever been ducked under water and held there, gasping for breath?"

"Yes, I have, and after I was pulled out, all I wanted was air," I said.

"Did you ever want your love as badly as you wanted air when you were in the water?"

"Yes, each time I loved intensely."

"Then why did it not work out?"

"I put my heart, soul, and mind into each relationship, and yet things did not go as planned. Perhaps, they were not meant to be."

"Did you plunge in love with a burning or fervent desire, as if little else mattered?"

"I did love as few could, and yet it wasn't as if anything else did not matter."

"As critically you wanted air after you were ducked underwater, so acutely should you pursue your love and desired profession," Dorothy said. "It is possible that the intensity of love and the yearning to cling to the beloved was missing in your relationships."

"Do you mean I gave a lot in love but did not desire it enough?" I asked.

"Yes. You have to plunge in love as if your world revolves around your heart's desire. In essence, you give in love, you invest in love, and you crave in love to stay devoted in love. That is the acme of adoration."

"I now know where I fell short in my relation-ships. I gave, I invested, and yet I did not crave enough," I replied.

"Señorita," the waitress interrupted. "Suprema de Pollo con Spaghetti a la Sorrentina."

With a beaming smile, she placed before us the delectable dish Dorothy had ordered for us. She then returned a minute later with the Donatello Sour to accompany the spaghetti. This was a perfect meal with a lovely lady. The way to a man's heart and the presence of an amazing woman were the ideal com-panions to enhance this momentous tryst.

We each took a few bites, and then Dorothy returned to our conversation.

"Occupation, vocation, or profession merits the same engrossed attention to attain preeminence. You may be good at what you do, you may be inter-ested in what you do, you may pour your feelings and mind into it, but what really matters is the intense desire to go beyond mastering your craft or aspiration. It is only when you strive to better what you have already attained as an expert in your field do you begin the process of creative obliteration."

"But why destroy what you've created after painstaking efforts and sacrifices?" I asked.

"Because true eminence is not just about reaching the apogee of fame or wealth. It is about rediscovery, relearning, and reinvention. It is about the master always staying a student. It is the point where the end and the beginning tango."

"You mean irrespective of the heights of greatness achieved, we should always strive to remain an interested, passionate, and intense student of our occupation or craft?"

"Exactly. The right to be the leading light of your professional pursuit is to carry on as a student."

The color of Dorothy's eyes had changed to dark green. Andrew had told me about this. Her sensuality was beginning to show through her soft features, profound words, magnetic eyes, and ethereal voice. Her presence illuminated the restaurant. It felt like pure magic. I had never met such a fascinating woman and was becoming irresistibly drawn toward her.

"What are you thinking about and why have you stopped eating?" she asked, obviously noticing that my mind had gone for a walk.

I was at loss for words. How do I confess to my

just discovered fascination for the exquisite Dorothy? How do I continue the conversation with a wandering mind? All I knew was that I had to figure out a way to meet her again. This could not be the last time.

"Why is the process of creative obliteration so important?" I asked to keep the conversation going.

"A genius never rests on his laurels. An achiever creates an object of ingenuity, and after its culmination reinitiates the process of creative construction that obliterates or disrupts previous triumphs. The past is left behind for a different, richer, and better today and tomorrow."

"So, as an analogy, if I authored a high-quality book that improves relationships among young people, my next book on relationships ought to be so much more superior that it relegates the first to oblivion."

"You got it. The journey from good to great lies in destroying what you zealously created by surpassing your previous creation time and again, and yet retaining the disposition of a novice."

I was beginning to understand why eminence had eluded me. While I had tasted success, the yearning to outstrip each of my creations and peaks had never occurred. Further, being famous and celebrated was more important than being top-notch or the very best in my work life.

"Go forth and relive an orgasm," Dorothy said.

"While making love, you experience the bliss of an orgasm. It is time you experience the orgasm of your craft just as you have experienced the orgasm of love. This time around, crave enough. Re-create or disrupt enough and excel enough."

Well, one thing was for sure. I wanted Dorothy enough. Sometimes all it takes is a conversation to be love-struck. I wanted to be the photographer who captured the ethereal Dorothy on film. I wanted to be the painter who created her priceless portrait. I wanted to be the writer who penned a novel about her captivating persona. I wanted to be her lifelong beloved.

Yet what stood between Dorothy and me was paucity of time. The lunch rendezvous was about to end, and I knew I had to find an excuse to meet her again. She had imparted invaluable lessons already, but that was not enough. I was beginning to fall in love with her and wanted to take my chances with wooing her. I also needed to find out why she had slipped away from Andrew's life. I owed that to Andrew. I may have been besotted by her, but it was Andrew's fascinating depiction of Dorothy that had ignited the quest to meet and know this exceptional facilitator of relationships.

The jigsaw puzzle of my early-morning dream was manifesting itself. Given the triumvirate of an exotic location, intriguing lady, and captivating conversation, I felt the world was at my feet, that nothing was impossible, that true love was in the air, and that the anointed date and time to eminence was moments away. In the past, the films *Forrest Gump* and *The Pursuit of Happyness* had inspired me to think in big, bold, and creative ways. For once, a remarkable woman's words were making me believe that life was waiting to happen. And I had to seize the moment to continue our conversation.

"I want to express my deep gratitude," I said, "and if I may, I would like to take you out to dinner by the Pacific Ocean."

Dorothy's gaze was fixed on me. From her eyes and expression, I saw that she knew I was genuine, yet she also recognized that the dinner invitation was not a mere gesture of appreciation.

"You want to meet me again," she said. "Your eyes are seeking an answer to a question of great consequence."

I was taken aback. Had she figured out my connection to Andrew?

"Dorothy, I owe an answer to someone very important in my life and only you have the key. So please accept the dinner request."

"You are determined to meet me again. Your eyes are beginning to look at me as few men do. They speak the truth, and yet they have more to solicit and convey. I don't know why, yet my eyes would like to meet you again. Very well. We will do dinner tomorrow at 8:30 p.m. at La Dama

Juana—the very restaurant at Larcomar where you eavesdropped on George and me. Dinner by the Pacific Ocean will hopefully provide all the answers your eyes are seeking."

As we parted for the day, I got a hug from Dorothy. Never had a hug felt so exhilarating and special.

The ecstasy of discovering the attractive woman of my recurring dream was indescribable. Yet I could not help but ponder over Dorothy's statement: "I don't know why, yet my eyes would like to meet you again."

Was Dorothy also beginning to fall in love with me? Did she fathom that there was more to our next rendezvous than the important answer I sought? My mind would not calm down, but I had to figure out a way to get Dorothy to divulge the reason behind her unexpected exit from Andrew's life. The biggest test of my life awaited me.

Only God knew if I would be a worthy heir to Andrew's legacy.

Five

Travel enables the formation of meaning-ful connections. However, a hand-of-destiny sojourn that unbelievably induces a captivating lady to walk out of a dream and appear in reality is the journey of a lifetime. What is it about an enchanting woman that can make you forget everything around you? What is it about a special woman that makes you want to stay in a state of compulsive fantasy? Sometimes a lovely woman's presence can make you tongue-tied. Sometimes it can make you chatty. Sometimes it can make you say things you had not envisaged or intended. Yet when there is a larger purpose to get the endearing lady to talk about something she may not be comfortable with, the challenge amplifies. I knew the answers I sought would require both tact and bold queries.

More often than not, each time I was caught up with a conundrum or a challenge, what bailed me out was the art of asking the right or difficult questions with dexterity. Fortunately for me, I had strengthened this attribute with repeated practice while working with my clients. The story of Dorothy and Andrew seemed to be shrouded in mystery. Andrew was a legendary relationship coach, yet how could such a celebrated coach be so clueless and powerless to allow his beloved Dorothy disappear? Was it the biggest paradox that even the ablest relationship guru would have at least one person in this world that he or she would not be able to entirely convince, persuade, or influence? The time had come to decipher the hidden truth with the unassuming art of inquisition.

At the back of my mind, I knew this investigative exercise would be one of the biggest tests of my life; and if I could get Dorothy to talk and reveal all, it would be the most significant moment of my relationship advisory practice and the perfect parting gift for Andrew.

That evening I pondered long and hard for possible ways and methods to get Dorothy to talk about Andrew. She was a very perceptive individual and would immediately decipher the purpose of my inquiry. I would have to be a creative query agent. Yet I did not find a potentially successful approach for Project Dorothy-Andrew Talk. The night and my hours of consideration had progressed well into the early hours of the morning with no luck or idea of the smartest way to get Dorothy to reveal the best kept secret of her life: Why had she walked away from Andrew's life?

I cannot remember when my eyes got heavy and I fell asleep. Dorothy's gaze and unusual words— "I don't know why, yet my eyes would like to meet you again"—had me spellbound. The next thing was a bolt from the blue. Our lips met. The meeting of our lips in a cadence made the beating of our two hearts in rhythm audible. Two souls had become one. There was music in the air. The fervent kiss continued for a few minutes, disrupted only because the longing to look at each other was intense. She grabbed my left hand and said, "Let us walk to the Pacific Ocean." Overcome by the moment of togetherness and Dorothy's exquisiteness, I smiled and, without uttering a word, walked hand in hand with her toward the blue beauty. The afterglow of a gaze, an adoring kiss, and a stroll with a fascinating lady called for a special silence in which to soak in the incomparable moment.

Just then my iPhone alarm began to buzz, and my morning dream was undesirably brought to an anticlimactic end. For a few minutes I refused to accept that Dorothy and I had kissed each other only in my dream. It had seemed so real that the morning appeared as a fantasy. I could not believe my deep, subliminal desire of embracing Dorothy had manifested itself in a dream. Yet I was aware that staying in a cloud-cuckoo-land contained an overpowering drive to turn fantasy into reality. I had to make it happen. I had to woo Dorothy. I had to touch Dorothy. For the first time in my life, I felt so different and so strong about a woman. I couldn't be wrong. Dorothy and I were meant to be together for life. But how could I make this happen? The million-dollar tactic still eluded me.

Sometimes the paralysis of analysis is an impediment because it leads to excessive thoughts, similar to junk mail that appears in an e-mail account. Sometimes it is best to look within for an answer to the biggest opportunities or roadblocks. Sometimes it helps to quieten the mind through meditation. Almost immediately, I closed my eyes and with an erect posture, sat cross-legged on the bed. At the onset, a thought parade did not help me focus on the solution. An endless gush of thoughts, positive and negative, had to play out. I allowed the thoughts to come and go. I did not block any thought. Slowly but surely a deep sense of calm prevailed, even as I felt I was connected to the Lord. An unseen voice said, "The jewels are within you. Let your honesty and sincerity show up."

Connecting with the purest source leads to the levity of mind and heart. The knotty becomes simple and effortless, and the smile is back on the face. Sometimes it is the simplest and yet forgotten axioms of life that have the answers to the most complicated situations. "The jewels are within you. Let your honesty and sincerity show up."

An hour later, I enjoyed a scrumptious breakfast, complete with fruit and juice. Most fruits and juices are light on the stomach. They remind me of living life light and not taking it too seriously.

Just then Anne Simpson, a friend, walked into the breakfast hall. I waved, and as she noticed my presence, she walked over and hugged me. "Mike," she said, smiling, "it is nice to see you. What are you doing in Lima?"

"Good to see you too. Anne, it's been ages since we met. How have you been?"

"I couldn't be better. Wonder of wonders that we have met in Peru, considering we never run into each other in Chicago."

Anne and I had been classmates at Northwestern University. We had not seen each other in years. The last I heard she was a marketing consultant with a top financial-services consultancy in Chicago.

"So what brings the marketing genius to Lima?" I asked.

"I'm here to undertake a marketing study on the microfinance business. Lima has a highly-developed financial services industry for the underprivileged, and it's considered among the best in the world. What impresses me most is the dogged character and incredible entrepreneurial spirit displayed by the people of the low income areas of the city. It's helped them work their way out of poverty with dignity and pride."

"What is the biggest lesson you've learned so far from your field trips in low-income areas?" I asked.

"They've taught me that even with little material comforts, they think differently and big. They've opened my eyes to a range of business ventures that operate out of diverse low-income areas. There are limitless options to explore as an entrepreneur.

"I've been at the Del Pilar Hotel for a week," she added. "Too bad we didn't meet earlier."

"Sometimes two friends stay in the same hotel in another country oblivious of each other's presence, only to have them connect over food," I said.

"I have to go now, but what are you doing this evening? Let's meet up for dinner."

"I am sorry, but I'm out for dinner," I replied. There was no way I would cancel my dinner date with Dorothy.

"No problem. Perhaps, we can meet up for a drink tomorrow evening."

"Let's play it by ear. I may be heading back home tomorrow. If not, I'll buzz you or leave a message at the front desk and we can catch up over drinks and dinner," I said.

"Sure. Look forward to seeing you tomorrow."

"Can you recommend any interesting place to visit or exciting thing to do in Miraflores before lunch?"

"Why don't you head for Tandem Paragliding? It's located at the Malecón Cisneros in Miraflores. The closest landmark is the famous Love Park, also known as Parque del Amor. The paraglides are guided by trained pilots, and you get this breathtaking aerial view of one of the most scenic landscapes of Lima. Soaring in the sky over the Pacific Ocean is an out-of-body experience. You'll love it." Anne got up from her chair to bid me good-bye for the day. A friend's hug later, I decided it was time to explore the adventurous side of Lima.

Shortly thereafter I was airborne with a certified pilot. Witnessing a beautiful and clear azure sky, I felt as if I was experiencing the expansiveness of the universe. The world beneath was so tiny. The cars, the houses, and the people looked like miniatures, like animated toys. I embraced the small world with my big open arms as the pristine wind kissed my cheeks—sheer bliss accompanied with an unfathomable serenity that I had not felt in a long time.

For the first time, my eyes, mind, heart, and body experienced paradise up in the open skies. I felt as if a bound and constrained being had been released, as if a chained mind and heart had been set free. An inhibited Michael Elliott had been liberated in the presence of the heavens above and the Pacific Ocean underneath. A catharsis was happening and something intuitive told me, "From here on, Mike, you will be soaring high. Your time has come."

Upon returning to the Del Pilar Miraflores Hotel, I received a note from reception that Andrew had left in my absence. The note said, *Mike, if you get the chance, please see me or speak with me before you return to Chicago.*

I hastened to my room to phone Andrew, but just as my index finger was about to dial the first digit of his number, I stopped myself. Should I tell Andrew that I had chanced to find Dorothy, which had led to a luncheon meeting? Should I inform him about my dinner date with her?

Wait a minute. I couldn't share Dorothy with anybody. Was I out of my mind?

But it was because of Andrew that I met Dorothy.

I was indebted to Andrew as the generous recipient of his legacy. I was beholden to him for telling me about the lovely Dorothy, and yet there was another truth that was more powerful than my predicament or sudden possessive streak. Dorothy had disappeared mysteriously from Andrew's life, and without understanding the reason behind her disappearance, it would be a folly to disclose to Andrew that I had found the *missing* Dorothy. The evening rendezvous with Dorothy would hopefully bring out the concealed reality. Thus, I thought it best not to return Andrew's call until the next morning.

One of the most important evenings of my life was merely a few hours away. *The jewels are within you.*

Let your honesty and sincerity show up. The wise words of my meditative inner voice were reassuring.

My deportment bore an aplomb I had not witnessed in years. The need to impress Dorothy or think of convoluted ways to bring up Andrew in conversation had dispersed. Yes, I wanted to confess my adoration to Dorothy and also hear her Andrew narrative, yet I was not edgy or apprehensive. Nothing is more alluring than self-confidence and discreet candor. *When you do not make an attempt to impress others or to express yourself, your impression is impressive and your expression is compelling.* It was a good time to get a power nap and recharge my fatigued body.

As I was about to doze off, the phone in my room started to ring.

"Señor, you have a call from Andrew. Should I connect you to him?"

Uh-oh, I thought.

Seconds later, Andrew greeted me on the phone. "Mike, is this a good time to talk?"

"Yes," I said.

"I left a message for you at the hotel. Did you receive it?"

"Yes, I did. I'm sorry I didn't return your call. I was meaning to do so later today."

"No problem. I just wanted to share with you the best-kept secret between Dorothy and me."

"You mean you know why Dorothy never saw you again?"

"No, I don't know the precise reason. But the secret may provide a clue. I want to tell you about it before you return to Chicago. Can we meet later tonight or tomorrow morning?"

I was sure about one thing. While a clue might be of help, if it was such important evidence, then surely Andrew would have figured it out. If I wished to get to the bottom of the secret and put the jigsaw puzzle together to help a dying man, I needed all the time that evening with Dorothy.

"Can we meet tomorrow at 11:30 a.m.?" I asked.

"That would be wonderful. Would you be able to swing by my place?"

"Yes. I will be there at 11:30."

"Mike, I cannot thank you enough. And I will tell you tomorrow why I didn't share the secret with you earlier."

Andrew had read my mind. I hesitated to ask him why now and not earlier. Yet I had to respect his reason for doing so and wait for tomorrow to present itself with Andrew's unwrapped version.

"Good-bye, Mike, and see you tomorrow."

For a fascinating lady to walk away from a special friendship is never easy. And Dorothy must have had a good reason to do so. I could sense regret in Andrew's voice. Perhaps he was on a guilt trip and needed to relieve himself of a burden. A dying man wants to pass away with a clear conscience. Andrew had not only chosen to bequeath his legacy to me, but also disclose possibly the most private and delicate matter of his life. It was important for me to put the mind clock to rest now, though. Only time would unravel the mystery, and the wait was only a night away. Nothing ought to undo the tranquility that had been gifted to me by the paragliding excursion.

A warm shower before an important engagement augments the optimistic spirit. The primary shower accouterments—soap, shampoo, and song—make the wet exercise distinctive. The lathered soap adds to the significance of smelling nice and feeling spotless. The lyrics sung with eyes closed, bubbly shampoo adorning the hair, makes the novice sound like a soloist. The body suddenly starts sparkling as much as a newly bought mirror. A hot shower does wonders—and almost instantaneously I felt that the evening of a lifetime had just commenced.

I reached La Dama Juana at Larcomar on time. A few minutes later a lady in a striking red dress with a low neckline entered the restaurant and walked by me. She paused for a second, turned around, and said, "Are you waiting for Dorothy Porter?"

I could not take my eyes off her - the lady in red was Dorothy.

"You look lovely, simply divine," I said, paying her a genuine compliment.

"Are you flirting with me?" she asked cheekily as she sat.

"I am simply stating the truth."

"So you wanted to meet me again. May I ask why?"

"Because I owe an answer to someone very important in my life, and only you have that answer."

"And may I ask who that very important person is?"

She was direct as direct can be. We were only in the first few minutes of our dinner, and yet the pace of the exchange was rather rapid for my comfort. I was not sure how she would react to Andrew's name and if it came up too early in the evening. It might mean an abrupt end to the dinner date. So I decided to slow the pace of this breakneck chat.

"I will come to that in a minute. Would you like to have a glass of wine?" I asked.

"White will be fine, thank you."

A glass of wine has the uncanny power of bringing comfort to a sensitive conversation. Once the comfort factor sets in, the conversation opens up and confidential issues are easily discussed, which makes for interesting heart-to-heart sessions.

"Dorothy, you are a very perceptive person."

"Thank you. I've always loved observing people, their conversations, their eyes, their spoken and unspoken words, their expressions and body language."

"Did you develop this discerning ability when you edited *People Mantra*?"

"*People Mantra* sharpened my people observation

skills. As an editor, it's important to ask the right questions and be a good listener. Listening honed my perceptive abilities."

"*People Mantra* made you famous. How did that magazine happen?" I asked.

"Andrew Smith, the owner of *People Mantra*, brought me in as the editor in chief."

"That was one of the best magazines on relationships. It did awaken America to look at relationships with fresh eyes."

"Andrew deserves the credit. He trusted me implicitly and gave the editorial team a free hand."

"Did you know Andrew prior to working with him on *People Mantra*?" I asked. The wine was working. Dorothy was warming up to her past and making my mission of uncovering the Andrew-Dorothy enigma easier.

"Yes, I did, as a senior communications professional with his PR firm."

"I heard he sold *People Mantra* to its employees and became a relationship coach."

"Surely you must have met him, as you are part of the same business?" asked Dorothy.

Much as I would have liked to, this was not an appropriate time to disclose that Andrew had invited me to Peru and his home. The game of chess between Dorothy and me had begun. I was once again reminded of the words of my marketing professor at Northwestern University: "Strategy and the game of chess are analogous. Don't make the first move till you have visualized and calculated your last move."

"I am told it was you who inspired him to become a relationship coach," I said, attempting to skirt her query.

"And may I ask where you heard that?"

"Amazing truths can never stay concealed."

From Dorothy's gaze, I knew she had begun to suspect I knew more than I was saying.

"You look celestial today," I said. "That is an incredible truth and nobody can deny it. Similarly, behind Andrew's success as a relationship adviser is a remarkable truth—Dorothy Porter."

"Should I thank you, ignore your flirtatious compliment, or dig deeper into your comment?"

"That is for you to decide," I said audaciously.

"I like men who are bold, but somehow I get the feeling you are here for more than one answer."

"And what makes you say so?"

"Your eyes do not lie and your final words from yesterday's lunch. 'Dorothy, I owe an answer to someone very important in my life and only you have the key."

My strategy was working. The timing was perfect. What was the well-kept secret of what happened between Dorothy and Andrew or what drove my fascination with Dorothy? Both questions needed answers, and hopefully honest and positive answers. Which question should I ask first? Andrew had bestowed his legacy on me, while Dorothy had conquered my heart. I knew that irrespective of the order of the query, I risked upsetting Dorothy and the possibility of her walking out. That could mean the end of the tryst and no answer to the second query.

So, it was Andrew or me. Once again the sagacious words of my meditative inner voice came to my rescue: *The jewels are within you. Let your honesty and sincerity show up.* It was a unanimous decision. The strength of character had to place Andrew before me.

"Why did you mysteriously disappear from Andrew's life?" I asked unequivocally, backed by the power of my sincerity.

"What happened between Andrew and me stays between us. I am sorry, but I do not like to talk about it," Dorothy said. Her expression indicated she was offended by my intrusive question.

"I am sorry for bringing this up. I respect your privacy and don't want to compel you to reveal a secret. But I owe this to a dying man who wonders why you departed from his life. He invited me to Lima and opened his heart out to me. He longs to know what went wrong."

"What? Andrew is dying!" Dorothy exclaimed in disbelief, even as tears began to roll from her eyes.

Unthinkingly, I wrapped my arms around her to

console her. She hugged me tight and began weeping. She cried like a baby oblivious of her surroundings. In her lamentation lay a deep affection for Andrew. Her heart was bleeding at the thought that Andrew was in his last days.

I had also witnessed the glow in Andrew's eyes when he spoke about Dorothy. If they shared such a deep-rooted connection, why did it snap so abruptly?

"Mike, can you drop me off at my home please?" Dorothy asked, still visibly upset. "I'm sorry, but I can't stay here anymore."

"Oh, please don't be sorry. I understand. Let's leave." I gestured to an attendant for the check.

The walk from the restaurant to the cab was only a short stroll, yet it felt like the longest walk I had taken in a while. Dorothy clung on to me as if I were her crutch. The emotive distance between us had shrunk; we were no longer mere acquaintances. Andrew had done me dual favors: he had bequeathed his legacy to me and, sadly but truthfully, learning his time was almost over had compelled Dorothy into my caring arms.

Life works in strange ways. I was staying in a hotel in Miraflores and, coincidentally, Dorothy's home was in Miraflores. The cab ride to her apartment took all of twenty minutes. For most of the journey home, she sobbed, allowing me to hold her in my arms. A few minutes before we reached her apartment building, she stopped crying yet did not say a word. The taxi driver stopped in front of the high-rise, she finally spoke.

"Would you like to come in for a cup of coffee?"

"Sure, as long as you sit and watch me make the cup of coffee," I said, smiling.

"You are a nice guy. Come in and impress me with your coffee skills."

The elevator ride to her seventh floor apartment took a mere fifteen seconds. She led me into her unpretentious yet tasteful living room. A quick glance summarized the furnishings: a black leather couch with side tables and lamps, a large flat-screen TV on one wall, two handmade Persian carpets, a mahogany bookshelf with what appeared to be over one hundred leather-bound books, a reproduction of the timeless *Mona Lisa*, embellished golden-silk curtains, a baby grand piano, and a welcoming fireplace.

Dorothy excused herself and headed to her bedroom. She required some private time to get hold of her emotions. While she was gone, I perused the bookshelf. William Shakespeare's masterpiece *The Merchant of Venice* caught my attention. I pulled it from the shelf and began to read the timeless classic. It felt great to revisit one of my favorite works of the great playwright.

A few years earlier, I had visited Shakespeare's birthplace, Stratford-upon-Avon, and had subsequently bought a collection of his thirty-seven plays—all of the comedies, histories, and tragedies.

"Shakespeare is the best and among all his plays, *The Merchant of Venice* is my favorite," Dorothy said as she walked into the living room and saw me perusing the play. After the initial shock, it appeared she had regained her composure.

"I couldn't agree with you more," I said.

"Portia and Antonio are fascinating characters."

"Well, I find you equally intriguing," I said as I walked closer to her.

"And may I ask what makes me intriguing?"

"I have never met such an exceptional, sensitive, wise, and attractive woman as you. Your eyes... I could gaze into them for hours."

Dorothy's eyes did not bat an eyelid. She looked intently as she walked toward me.

"You have an uncanny ability to get a man thinking about you twenty-four seven," I went on. "Once a discerning man has indulged in a meaningful conversation with you, he cannot forget you. From then on, the roots of your being are deeply planted in him."

"Mike, how deep is deep?" Dorothy whispered in my ear.

"As deep as the profound truths of life and as unfathomable as my adoration for you," I replied. I began to stroke her glistening hair. She did not stop me.

"Mike, you remember I told you the last time we met that I didn't know why, yet my eyes would like to meet you again? Your eyes speak the truth. I see an unusual human being who can love as few can, yet he is looking for true love. Well, my eyes want to meet your eyes." She inched closer until there was no distance between us.

Our lips met. We kissed softly with her eyes closed and her arms wrapped around my neck. My hands continued to caress her hair. The morning dream had become a reality. Sheer magic... "The meeting of our lips in a cadence made the beating of our two hearts in rhythm audible. Two souls had become one. There was music in the air. The fervent lip-lock continued for a few minutes being disrupted only because the longing to look at each other was rather intense."

It was time to move to her room. Two intense and experienced individuals intertwined in passionate lovemaking were beginning to discover each other. The toned man and the voluptuous lady could not take their hands off each other. They explored every inch of their undressed bodies without inhibitions. They conceived postures and experimented galore. They gave and received abundant pleasure. They tickled and laughed together, they drank together... and they forgot Andrew together.

I had never slept with a woman as exquisite as Dorothy. The electrifying union with her was special because of a wordless emotional connection I had struck with her during the lovemaking. Between lust and love, there is a fine line of differentiation, and that night our irresistible attraction for each other had culminated into *dearly loved.*

I don't recollect when we fell asleep, but I do remember that Dorothy had snuggled into my arms and I planted a few kisses on her forehead. She seemed to be at peace with herself and I was on top of the world because of the veracity of that early-morning dream. Dorothy and the Pacific Ocean were working in symphony to change my life forever.

Next morning, I woke up to find Dorothy was not lying beside me. *She must be in the shower,* I told myself. I was exulting in the afterglow of the best night of my life as I waited patiently for her to appear all freshened up from the shower. The wait continued, and yet Dorothy did not come out of the bathroom.

Time for me to join her in the shower, I thought impishly. Seconds later I knocked on the bathroom door, but got no reply. I knocked once again, only to have silence greet me. There was no sound of running water either. I called out Dorothy's name; no response. Without any further wait, I barged into the bathroom only to see my face in the mirror. Dorothy was not there.

She must be in the kitchen, perhaps preparing breakfast for me. I dashed into the kitchen. Not a soul in there. I had passed the living room, and there too there was no trace of her. At that moment, it dawned on me that she must have stepped out of her apartment for an errand and would return soon.

I walked back to her room. After a quick shower, as I started to dress, I noticed a writing table in the corner of the room. In the heat of the night, I had failed to notice it.

On the desk was an envelope marked "For Michael." A pen had been left on top as a paper-weight. I hurriedly opened the envelope to see a handwritten letter by Dorothy addressed to me.

> *Dear Mike,*
>
> *Thank you for touching me as you did last night. You made me feel like the most wanted and beautiful woman in the world. The sincerity that I saw in your eyes when you implored me over lunch to meet you again was rather alluring. And your persistence to seek the answer for Andrew may have meant encroaching on my privacy, yet I find your pushiness laudatory as you did it for a dying man whom you do not know very well.*
>
> *I will always cherish the moments we spent together. You have the makings of an extraordinary partner, and yet the time to bid good-bye has come. I am aware that you are*

*deeply in love with me, and that it is equally
important for you to attain greater heights as a
relationship coach. Eminence in this profession
can only come through single-minded pursuit of
your goal devoid of any distractions. I may have
similar feelings for you, but considering your
giving nature, you would be consumed by my
physical presence in your life, which to my mind
you can ill afford at this crucial juncture.*

*The biggest diversion of your life… Dorothy will
become your biggest impediment on the road to
illustriousness. You would stay so wrapped up
in my adoration, you would not be able to focus
on taking your relationship-advisory practice
to its logical conclusion—the acme of global
prominence. With all humility at my command,
I make the aforesaid observations, because
sincere, intelligent, and loving individuals like
you who also harbor big dreams have often
disregarded their ambitions at the altar of
true love, only to find themselves living with
unfulfilled desires, or professional frustrations
that surface much later and invariably destroy a
delightful relationship.*

*True love does not bind or impede. It does not
come in the way of progress. As much as I would
love for us to be together, I would abhor the
thought of an unusual talent such as you staying
largely unnoticed because of the inevitable.*

Our love, time, and happy moments together would most definitely become more important than your career. That would be such a loss to the world, which needs a wonderful individual and exceptional relationship coach to illuminate broken hearts and strengthen the relationships of thousands of people across the world.

You may argue that we could strike a fine balance between our love and your career and you can still make it big, but for a benevolent individual like you, balance can be the biggest obstacle to professional augmentation. The only way forward is imbalance… without any attachments.

Only two men have touched my life in a very special way and coincidentally, they both belong to Chicago. Andrew was the first and you the second.

Andrew and I worked together for a few years, and when the professional relationship turned into an amazing union of mind and body, I became his weakness and not a source of strength. He became so emotionally dependent on me that his new role as a relationship coach did not take off as well as People Mantra did. He risked going downhill from there, and despite my repeated requests that he focus on his career,

I—as his soft spot—had become his biggest barrier to noteworthy progress.

I loved Andrew dearly and I could not see his growth come to a halt. True love is altruistic. It gives at the cost of accepting the pain of separation. It was time to move on. It was time to move far away from Andrew, to another country. Lima was an ideal choice, considering that I was an unknown entity here and my mother lived in Peru. I departed with an ardent belief that in my exit lay a blessing that would lead to Andrew's meteoric rise as a relationship coach of distinction. And it happened as rapidly as People Mantra's ascent. Andrew became the best-known relationship coach, and each time he was lauded in the media, I watched and hugged him from a distance. I resolved not to meet Andrew again because love does get in the way of advancement.

History is repeating itself. Today, you are where Andrew was some years ago, and I am sure you will go places as a relationship coach sans my physical presence. Once again the time to part ways has come.

I love you immensely and ask for your forgiveness to accept my selfless explanation. You may not comprehend the rationale of my good-bye, and yet I am confident that in time to come you will recognize the merit of my argument. With a heavy heart, I write this note and bid you good-bye—and to request a favor from you. Please do not meet me again until such time as you have realized your dream or try to convince me to change my mind. You now know where I stay, and yet I can only urge you not to visit me again or share my apartment address with Andrew. You wanted an answer for him as much as he wanted to know the reason for my unexpected departure. I leave it to your discretion to share this note with him. I will meet him soon, for he needs to live and die in peace and without any guilt or regret.

Last night was beautiful. I will miss you, but from here on, for every accolade, triumph, struggle, or disappointment, I will be with you in spirit. You just have to close your eyes, feel my presence, and you will find me with you and around you.

Hugs, kisses and smiles for a great future.

Dorothy

I could not believe what I had just read. I felt as if an arrow had pierced my heart. The letter and the wounded heart hurt terribly. Dorothy had just entered my life, and after the perfect night she had left me with a tearful letter of sacrifice, love, and separation.

For the first time I despised my ambition of the pursuit of eminence. For the first time I wanted to leave it all for a fascinating woman. After all, what was the point of attaining happiness and enormous success if it couldn't be shared with somebody special? I wept as a child, and only after a half hour was able to end the gush. Just then, I realized that Dorothy was right! I was ready to give it up all for her. I was ready to forsake my dreams and ambitions to have her in my life. Her captivating persona would be a source of great delight, yet it would truly be the biggest distraction and would mar my professional journey. And truly, it was in her sacrifice that my journey to fulfilling prominence would be possible. Dorothy's prudence, judgment, and generosity of spirit were indeed commendable. Mike, the unimportant relationship coach, had learned the defining lesson of his trip to Lima.

Upon returning to the Del Pilar Miraflores Hotel, I headed to my room to change into a fresh pair of clothes—khaki trousers and sky-blue T-shirt. I had to make a significant visit to Andrew's home shortly. The answer to Andrew's inquisition was no longer a mystery. I did not need a clue anymore. Andrew and I could have been competitors in love, but our love and beloved was merely beyond carnal possession. Andrew, the dying luminary, and I, the new kid on the block, had something to read together. The most valuable letter of our lives was waiting to see its most fitting suitors together.

I reached Andrew's apartment on time. I had a solitary travel companion—Dorothy's unforgettable letter. Andrew greeted me with an infectious smile and asked if I would like a cup of tea or coffee. I chose the stronger option, coffee. I wanted to stay energized for what might be a cathartic moment for Andrew.

Over coffee, I handed Dorothy's letter to Andrew. It would tell Andrew everything he wanted to know. Sometimes it is best to let the written word do the talking. Minutes later, as his eyes got watery, the first tear trickled down his cheek. At the end of the letter he closed his moist eyes and said, "Dorothy, the only thing you know is to sacrifice and give. I owe the world to you. My final desire before I go to meet my maker will at last be fulfilled. You will finally meet me. Thank you. I can now die in peace."

He extended his hands and exhorted me to hold them. "Mike, you are indeed the suitable inheritor to my legacy. I cannot thank you enough. Your fascination for Dorothy did not override the answer I sought from her. In one night, you spent a lifetime with her, and yet you chose to come over and share a very private and sensitive letter with me. I am endlessly grateful to you."

Andrew opened his tearful eyes and continued,

"I want you to make a promise. You will not let Dorothy's sacrifice go in vain. You will become the most renowned relationship coach the world has ever known. A dying man blesses you in abundance. You are a good man."

He kissed my hands, held them tight, and started to weep. I too could not hold my tears back. Two relationship coaches who loved the same woman started to cry together – their bond with the spell-binding Dorothy was a saga of extraordinary love that had been set free, because their exceptional ability to mend broken hearts and strengthen relationships would not reach its pinnacle had Dorothy decided to choose love over their careers.

The paradox of love. We could not mend Dorothy's broken, sacrificing heart because of our true calling, yet we had the innate ability to ameliorate the lives and relationships of strangers.

A universal truth: no matter how smart, spiritual, influential, or successful you may be, there is always that one person in your life who cannot be convinced, persuaded, or won over.

Andrew hugged me tight. We both knew this was our last meeting. I was too emotionally choked up to talk and clasped him tight to express my gratitude. It was the toughest moment of my life—to say goodbye to a dying man who had in the last few days handed me priceless treasures, enough to last a lifespan. I had found eternal love and a rich legacy in

Lima. Andrew had found an heir and the invaluable answer that eluded him for years. I wonder what Dorothy had found.

As I said good-bye, I knew and felt, and Andrew told me he felt the same way- Dorothy's compelling last words of her unforgettable letter, "I will be with you in spirit. You just have to close your eyes, feel my presence, and you will find me with you and around you."

The time to end a momentous journey had come. Christened by its Spanish founders as the City of Kings, Lima had truly lived to its name. Like a benevolent ruler, it had bestowed treasured jewels: the Pacific Ocean, Andrew's invitation to carry on his legacy, the attractive woman in white, the hugs, the touches, the conversations, and the magic union with a fascinating lady were all a bouquet of the incomparable memories I would take back with me to Chicago.

SIX

O n board the return flight from Jorge Chávez International Airport to Miami International Airport, en route to Chicago, I could not help but reflect on my conversations with Andrew and Dorothy, and their narratives. A pensive excursion that relives key moments of a miraculous trip ought to be put in writing. On my laptop, I noted the key points shared so generously by Dorothy and Andrew. I remembered verbatim what they both eloquently verbalized, each word so overwhelmingly powerful and unforgettable.

These priceless annotations would serve as points of reference and also help me revisit the special moments of a marvelous trip that had redefined the meaning of intimacy, magnanimity, and inheritance. My contemplative mind continued to go over the events that had unfolded most unexpectedly over the last few days: Andrew's surprise invitation as he chose me as the fitting inheritor of a legacy that could have been lost altogether. Dorothy's poignant letter took me back to that fairy-tale-like night where she and I had become one. I retraced every word, touch, and emotion, and the intensity of it all. Two deeply connected individuals would always have a telepathic connection. Dorothy had not left me or abandoned me. I could feel her presence around me. True love does not get better than this.

The long travel time and the layover flew by, and as the flight from Miami descended at O'Hare Airport, a bumpy landing nudged me out of the Lima trance. It was 5:15 p.m. Welcome back to Chicago, Mike. A new life beckons you. I could perceive the bounce in my feet. I was ready to spread my wings, buoyed by the insightful mantras acquired from Dorothy and Andrew. My time had come.

Chicago, arguably the architectural capital of the United States, would be the architect of my comeback. The time for a complete overhaul of my relationship practice had taken root in my mind. I kept remembering Andrew's tearful parting comment: "I want you to make a promise. You will not let Dorothy's sacrifice go in vain. You will become the most renowned relationship coach the world has ever known." I closed my eyes and made a promise to my inner self on behalf of Andrew, Dorothy, and me: Michael Elliott, you will become the world's most famous relationship coach, for you are preordained to strengthen human bonds and associations.

There is something special about coming back to your apartment. *Home sweet home.* You can travel the world, live in the best hotels, dine at the most exquisite restaurants, experience the most extraordinary moments of your life miles away from your abode, and yet home coming after all that is unmatched. The inviting door longs for you to insert your key and be welcomed into the comfortable living room; the lights long to bring brightness to your dwelling; the walls long to hear you talk to yourself; the couch longs to take your weight as you sit to unwind at the end of a trip; the television longs to disseminate news and be heard; the shower longs to hear you sing as you lather up, notwithstanding your inharmonious voice; and the familiar bed longs to put you in deep slumber to take away all the exhaustion of the long journey.

At home, you can be and stay yourself as you can seldom be anywhere else. It felt great to be back in the warm home that I called my own. I chose to resist the temptation of reading a book, watching a movie, or putting my feet up with a glass of Scotch. All these allurements would mean a very late night and an equally late start in the morning, something I could ill afford to do. After all, tomorrow would be the first morning of my reemergence, and an early start to strategize my resurrection would lead to its early implementation.

My fatigued body got its much needed rest, and when I woke up at 8:15 a.m., it was brimming with the energy that accompanies a man when he is out on a date with a pretty lady. After my shower, I decided to drive to Le Peep restaurant in Evanston for a wholesome breakfast. That would be followed by a daylong renaissance planning exercise on the beautiful campus of Northwestern University. Given that I had attended graduate school there, I had an emotional connection with it. I had even written most of the first draft of my book on campus.

Even though I had an office in the scenic Lincoln Park neighborhood, nostalgia and inspiration drew me to campus each time I needed to come up with something remarkable or different. Thus, it was logical to go back to my alma mater for brainstorming my next steps.

Le Peep brought back special memories of breakfast trips to the restaurant with former classmates who had become close friends. Delectable food, friendly banter, and endearing conversations would fill the air with laughter and joy. Upon graduation and just before we left campus for our respective worlds, some of my dear friends and I had congregated at Le Peep for our last breakfast together.

Post-breakfast, the walk from Le Peep to Norris University Center at Northwestern University took barely ten minutes. Norris, the center of campus life, was the place I would go to brainstorm when I was a graduate student.

Northwestern University had once breathed new life into my career, and history would repeat itself, except that what I envisaged and had to act on was bigger than anything I had done in the past. I was here to commence working on a business plan that would make me the most celebrated relationship coach for young people.

A business plan for a relationship-advisory practice sounds inane. However, writing a plan that would be the amalgam of Andrew's last wish, Dorothy's sacrifice, and my grand dream was imperative. It would be the document that would pull together all the disparate aspects and reflections into a strategic framework that would augment my coaching initiative.

Thanks to Dorothy and Andrew, I had a wealth of new insights. But I had a glaring weakness. I was the person who had to market my business, yet I could not effectively sell or promote myself simply because I was always uncomfortable talking ad nauseam about my work or myself. For an entrepreneur or self-employed professional, it was important to continually promote yourself, your activities, products, or services. Given that I found it difficult to belabor my work or myself, perhaps I had to hire somebody to talk about me. I could hire a public-relations agency to aggressively promote my profile and work with the media.

In the business plan, I thought it appropriate to assign a big budget for hiring a PR firm. I smiled. It would make me the next big thing in the world of relationship coaching.

Never before had I enjoyed a business plan exercise as I did that day. The plan may have been about formulating a framework for my business that required putting together strategy, tactics, budget, and numbers, yet it did not for once seem cumbersome or demanding. Dorothy's omnipresence and Andrew's last words kept me going.

With the assistance of a highly recommended business-plan software, I had by the evening created a plan that would leverage new-age marketing, communications and social media practices to rebuild my relationship-coaching business. No more was it just about me. It was more about the promise I had made to Andrew and to live up to the sacrifice made by Dorothy.

The most ambitious endeavor of my career now had a blueprint. Time had flown that day, as it had when I was a student on campus. The only difference was that I had not met a Dorothy Porter then. I had been in love before, but never had it felt so intense. Never before had I felt unimaginable enjoyment while drawing up a business plan as I did on that day at Norris Center. I had taken the first baby step toward my rebirth.

A day of new beginnings, a day of fulfillment, and a day of imaginative quest. The pleasure of attainment was inexplicable. It could only be expressed over a chilled beer at Tommy Nevin's Pub, one of the most frequented watering holes in Evanston. An Irish Pub, Tommy Nevin's used to be the default destination for my friends and me for a late bite and brew. Ten minutes later, a chilled Heineken in my right hand, I looked at the striking green bottle and remarked to myself, *Mike, you deserve the Heineken after a rewarding day. Cheers to the best relationship coach the world is about to set its eyes on.*

A few sips later, I couldn't help but think of some of the most cherished offerings and predilections that had enriched my life over the last few days: Pisco Sour and Heineken, the Pacific Ocean and Northwestern University, Evanston and Miraflores, Andrew and Dorothy. It was a blend of history, leisure, expansiveness, knowledge, emotions, memories, profundity, giving, and beauty. Such an unbelievable fusion of rewards does not happen to every individual. I had experienced the splendor of life and I could connect the dots. I could link the seemingly incongruent occurrences of the past, which had taught me that when life does not go as envisioned, it throws up something bigger and better. That was what made life such a celebration, and that was what made my drink so complete and refreshing.

As I enjoyed a plate of fries with my bottle of beer, the philosopher in me digressed to start counting the best "first" moments of my life.

- Realization of gender difference. In preschool, I first realized that the girls had longer hair than us boys. That meant we were different.

- Act of philanthropy. Out of the $100 I got as a gift from my grandparents on my seventh birthday, I gave $50 for charity at my Mom's request. She wanted to instill in me compassion for the underprivileged.

- Kiss. We were middle-school classmates who were extremely attracted to each other. She was clearly the cutest girl in the world then.

- Train trip. From Chicago to Michigan. It was the most unforgettable train journey of my life. My father asked me to use my imagination and write an essay that summarized that journey. It was an eventful trip simply because through the essay, my strong imagination was identified, which in years to come would help me as an author and creative professional.

- Teen date. Our neighbor's daughter's blue eyes asked me out, and we surreptitiously met for a movie and more. A pity they moved out of the suburb a few months later.

- Computer purchase. Entirely funded by garage sale earnings of my old camera, video games, and guitar. I got my first computer thanks to my valuable old companions.

- Visit to a golf course with my dad. He was the big boy in the bankers' golf circuit. After all, he got a hole in one on one of the toughest golf courses in the United States.

- Tennis trophy that I won after a lot of sweat. I came from behind to beat my closest competitor in a thrilling three-set final. He charmed away my girlfriend; I took away his dream trophy.

- Business. Rent-a-Book-a-Week made me enough money to fund an old Hummer and my college education, given that I was never a brilliant student.

- Car. A used but mind-blowing Hummer. The black beauty did help me woo a lot of pretty young ladies.

- Drink. A glass of Scotch with my dad, who enjoyed his whiskey. He always told me, "Son, your first drink and coming-of-age conversation should be with me. As you get older, you and I will continue to share a very special bond."

- Overseas trip. The United Kingdom was special, and Stratford-upon-Avon was an incredible journey. The greatest playwright, William Shakespeare and I share one thing in common—our love for words.

- Article published in a national magazine. The first feature story written by me that was published by one of the most reputable magazines of the country.

- Harley-Davidson. Given to me by my wonderful parents. One of the most precious possessions of my life, it taught me that style is eternal.

- Loan. A $2,000 loan to a financially distraught friend. I have not gotten the money back, but we are still friends.

- Visit to Northwestern University. The moment I drove onto the campus, I knew I would attend graduate school at the fabled university.

- Website content written by me. For my first employers, a consultancy company. It opened my mind to the amazing world of Internet and global connectivity. As a result, I designed the product strategy of a virtual credit card for a bank client, thanks to my understanding about websites and the Internet.

- Appearance on television. My expert opinion

on strategic marketing and communications was sought for a prime-time TV show.

- Press conference. The first press conference that I led got a lot of positive media attention for my employers.

- Book that sold on Amazon. As a first-time author, nothing gave me more delight than to see the first copy being sold on Amazon.

- Book signing. At a bookstore in downtown Chicago, where it felt special to be reading an excerpt from my book and signing copies for readers who had bought the book.

- Client. When I opened my doors as a relationship coach, I signed up my first client in a *bar*. That evening, under the influence of alcohol, I was impressive enough to convert a prospective into a client.

- Momentous trip. Lima was the epochal trip where I found it all.

In my inventory of the first and finest moments of my life that I went through that evening at Tommy Nevin's, I considered all the women I had been involved with. Barring the introductory phase of dating, I was not into casual relationships. For me each relationship meant being in love. I had loved five times, but each time had been unsuccessful in converting the dating relationship into matrimony.

The same story had repeated itself five times over. The initial year of the relationship was magic. I was a great guy, a die-hard romantic, and a thorough gentleman. Then the expected happened. Each of the five women dumped me because none of them was comfortable with my big dreams and plans. I loved to take professional risks, and they were risk averse. They had the luck yet could not dream big or take risks. I didn't have the luck, yet I thought bold and king-size because I knew that with resolve, I could change my luck.

They wanted me to stay in a job and live in the comfort zone of a six-figure salary. I wanted to experience life in its enormity and realize all my dreams. They did not want me to experiment with my professional choices, and the only way I knew to grow was to experiment. The five women I was deeply involved with were all from different ethnicities, but they had some things in common—a deprived upbringing, an advanced degree that led to a good job with a good salary, a passion for sport, long and beautiful hair, a beautiful smile, and a short temper.

I came from a privileged upbringing, but they had been raised with few material pleasures. Perhaps it was natural for them to want the best in life without taking too many risks. After all, if a six-figure salary could provide them with all the material razzmatazz they had longed for as children, why would they want to live with financial hardship?

That could be the case with a risk-taking partner. And as I had predicted, each of these five lovely ladies went on to marry rich guys.

The moment we went our separate ways, I severed my ties with all of them. Later, when I got some small fame, three of them reached out to me by sending Facebook friend request, which I declined. I had no hard feelings; I just did not see them as a part of my life. I had loved each of them dearly, but had not been fortunate enough to find love with an understanding partner who would support my dreams, as I would hers.

Reminiscing about the past was important before a new start. It reminded me of the ebb and flow of life's multihued experience. With folded hands, I thanked God profusely for staying with me through the ups and downs, and more importantly for Lima. I knew my life was about to change drastically.

The next morning, I reviewed my business plan. A few modifications later, I started to research the top public relations and marketing firms in Chicago that had experience with promoting a consultant, an author, or an individual. The key was to hire an agency that would build me as the preeminent relationship coach for young people. After a few hours of searching on Google and LinkedIn, I had drawn up a list of nine agencies that had the credibility, experience, and size to strategize and implement large-scale publicity. Later that day I sent out e-mails to the agencies with an outline of my profile and a request for an appointment to explore the possibilities of working together.

As I had expected, the next morning I received a reply from four agencies expressing an interest in taking me on as a client. Over the next two days I exchanged phone calls and e-mails with the agencies, sharing my objectives so they could come up with an inventive public-relations proposal.

The next stage was to meet each of them at my office, listen to their ideas, and subsequently make a choice. After nine hours of deliberations, the time for selection had come. The differentiating factor was in People Renaissance's presentation. They wanted to "reposition" me as the relationship coach for the "holistic young." The key attributes of the people in this segment were that they were educated, confident, assertive, and ambitious; and they enjoyed reading and social media, smart phones, tablets, and e-book readers. People Renaissance won my conviction and account.

I felt happy and strange at the same time. Happy because I had taken the first big step to fulfill my promise to Andrew and Dorothy; and strange because I, a communications expert who had created brands out of individuals and organizations, had signed up with a renowned marketing agency to shape his future. The paradox of my life: I could use deft communications strategies to make a brand of almost anybody except myself. I was paying out of my pocket to get an associate to sing my praises, and yet I called myself humble and modest. I could not stop laughing at myself, but I knew this step was absolutely necessary in a short-attention-span and preoccupied world.

People Renaissance wanted to use my book as a backdrop to resurrect my career. I sought out glowing book reviews and customer reviews and gladly provided the agency with them. The agency would get a detailed publicity plan to me in a week.

When a man finds true love and the beloved becomes his greatest inspiration to rise to the top of his profession, an air of infectious buoyancy spurs each thought and action. Dorothy had changed me. I was surer of myself than ever before. And my eyes shed a bigger tear than they ever had in the past. A tear that would commonly be associated with pain was, on the contrary, a tear of rapture.

The struggles of the past, the gargantuan grind to make a big difference, and the noble intention to enhance the lives of many had not been clearly understood by most people close to me, but that tear of joy cleansed the bag of pain I'd been carrying for a long time within my deepest recesses.

Just then, I realized that delayed attainment of what you truly deserve heightens the gratification of the success. I could not stop crying. I wept as a child with nobody except the invisible Almighty and my living room to witness my joy at the inevitable. What I had waited for was, I knew, just around the corner.

It is strange but true that when you are on the verge of colossal success, small things bring distinctive pleasure. The whiff of brewed tea becomes an olfactory delight; the razor that runs across a layer of gel on the cheeks appears to give the smoothest shave; the burger and fries with a cold soda is a piece of heaven; and a boat ride to revisit the skyline of Chicago is to witness life in all of its magnificence.

Something had changed. I had begun to understand that happiness lay in being able to enjoy the small with the big. Often in pursuit of bold dreams, we forget to appreciate that it is the small things in life, the mundane activities and chores, that build the foundation for enormous attainments. Without the small, the big is not possible. This is a key attribute for a joyful life. The lessons of Lima were slowly tiptoeing out of my computer to create a lasting transformation.

That night I could not stop thinking about Dorothy. A glass of premium Scotch and soft romantic music accentuated my longing to see her. I was, after all, human enough to want to stroke her hair, even if all we did was indulge in conversation. The most unforgettable night of my life at Dorothy's dwelling in Lima seemed like it had happened yesterday. Everything that had transpired between us was as fresh as the last sip of an aged Scotch.

During our intimate moments, her repeated avowals that she loved me had been music to my ears. My honest confession— "You are the most mesmerizing woman I have ever known"—drew out her sensual best for as long as possible. That night was all about giving because there was no receiver. That night was all about fulfillment of the destined. That night was all about an extraordinary lady leading me to a new beginning. The world did not exist for us. The dissimilar heart and head converged as aspirations were put to rest… and none but time witnessed unconditional love and an ocean of oneness.

Through my glass of Scotch, an unusual contradiction of my life stared at me. Had my ambition been pocket-sized, I would not have to stay away from Dorothy, yet it was because of my bold goal that Dorothy had decided to stay away from me.

Life is a tradeoff. You get plenty, but you do not get it all. I had received the legacy of Andrew, but I had to forgo Dorothy's physical presence in order to have that prized inheritance.

Alas, I could no longer speak to or touch Dorothy, yet the last words of her letter brought a tranquil acceptance to my soul. "Last night was beautiful. I will miss you, but from here on, for every accolade, triumph, struggle, or disappointment, I will be with you in spirit. You just have to close your eyes, feel my presence, and you will find me with you and around you."

SEVEN

"Hi Mike, this is Sheryl Cooper from People Renaissance. How are you doing today?"

"I couldn't be better. Thank you." I had answered the phone as I gorged on a bagel and cheese omelet for breakfast.

"Well, the PR plan is ready, and if you have some time today, we can go over it," Sheryl said.

"Will noon work for you?"

"Sure. Should we meet at your office or ours?"

"Your office, if that's possible," I replied.

"Great. I look forward to our discussion later today."

Sheryl had called me less than four days after our last meeting, following the general marketing dictum and relationship strengthener that recommended to underpromise and overdeliver. So this quick response had been expected, yet I nonetheless sensed a superior communication system with

People Renaissance. I had some interesting thoughts of my own for promoting my profile through online marketing and communication campaigns; however, it was best to keep that under wraps until I had seen People Renaissance's proposal.

At the agreed-on time, I reached the office of People Renaissance. Sheryl greeted me in reception and then accompanied me to the conference room. There I met her colleague Meher Gandhi, who hailed from India. She had graduated with a communications major from an Ivy League school, and for the last three years had made Chicago her home.

Meher looked taller than the average Indian woman. She had been a nationally ranked tennis player and attributed her success to her height, which was five feet, eight inches. Observing an unusual glow on her face, I intuitively felt there was something enigmatically distinctive about Meher.

Meher was the PR specialist for books and individually owned consultancy businesses. Over the next forty-five minutes, she made an eloquent presentation that consisted primarily of a few customary initiatives as well as some unusually different ones. She had also anticipated my questions and answered them all even before I had raised them.

I requested some quiet time to mull over the presentation. An hour later, after I had dissected every idea, I called Meher and told her I was ready to talk.

A minute later she walked into the conference

room with a beaming smile and cheekily said, "Trust me on this one, Mike. You will be huge after this PR campaign."

"I'm in your hands, Meher."

"This is the biggest challenge of my life, and nothing will give me more pleasure than seeing you reach your objective."

"That is very reassuring. Thank you."

"Don't you worry. You just hired the finest agency. We will keep you very busy too. Expect to hear from me tomorrow morning with the initial media pitch. Combine that with savvy story placement, and the PR campaign will be a success."

Meher's poise and positive energy convinced me that I had started in the right direction. There was also something about her reflective brown eyes that made me feel Meher had an interesting life story that was waiting to be shared.

Would the young PR maestro sign up as a client with the relationship coach for the holistic young? That would not be preposterous. After all, no matter how professionally competent we are, in our personal lives we all have a few cobwebs that need to be swept away.

True to Meher's word, the next morning I received in my inbox the draft media pitch with a list of the target audience—prominent print, broadcast, and online media companies that normally covered youth-oriented topics, such as lifestyle, careers, and relationships. In her e-mail, Meher stated, "It is important we target well-known reporters and editors, including influencers. It is better to get small coverage with one of the big five than a half page exposure in a lesser known newspaper or magazine. The same logic works for television and radio." She ended with: "The next time we meet, please autograph my copy of your book. When you become famous, I may not be able to get hold of you. At least I will be able to hold your autographed book."

A little tweaking later, I e-mailed the pitch back to Meher with a few additions to her list of targeted media. She requested I send her fifty copies of my book that could be forwarded to those reporters and editors who responded to the media pitch. This would provide the necessary ingredients for an interesting feature story.

A few hours later a box containing fifty copies of my book was dispatched to Meher via FedEx. In the box I added a handwritten note addressed to her— "I will autograph a copy of the book on one condition. I buy you lunch or dinner and you tell me your life story. Something tells me you need to talk and share. I am a good listener."

Meher called the next day, while I was at my office. "Mike, I got the box of books and your note. So, are you a better listener or relationship coach?"

"If you're hiring me, then I would have to be good at both," I said.

"Are you promoting your services to a PR specialist?"

"No, I'm making an exception to offer my ear to an ally who has a story to share."

"What makes you think I want to talk and share?"

"I can read eyes, and your eyes tell me you're nursing a wound."

"There's a wall as big as the Great Wall of China between my personal life and our professional association. Personal secrets should stay confidential and not have any bearing on the nature of your relationship with People Renaissance." Her emphatic voice spoke clear and loud.

"You have my word," I said. "Your story will go to my grave with me and will not in any way affect our professional association."

"Well, in that case, you have to autograph my copy of your book."

I chuckled. "I'll be doing you a favor. The value of the autographed book is going to double."

Meher laughed. "And I'm giving you the privilege of taking me out for dinner tonight."

"The honor is entirely mine."

We decided to meet at 8:30 at Bombay Chopsticks, located at Hoffman Estates. It served distinct and contemporary Indo-Chinese cuisine. The appetizers we ordered included delicious vegetable spring rolls and golden fried baby corn. This was followed by the main course, comprising Bombay Chopsticks' hakka noodles and cottage cheese with Manchurian sauce. The lip smacking delicacies and a succulent mango shake led to satiated stomachs, and made it easy for Meher to tell her heartrending story.

"Seven years ago," she began, "I worked for a well-known PR firm in New Delhi. I fell in love with a colleague, Rishi Singh, who was two years younger than I and given to extravagant living."

Entranced by Meher's adorable Indian accent, I listened intently.

"He loved me immensely, and when I was transferred to our employer's headquarters in Mumbai, he decided to request for a transfer too. Around the same time, Rishi's dad lost a huge amount of money in his real-estate business. From the lavish lifestyle that Rishi and his family were used to, came a descent into the depths of material destitution that was devoid of their retinue of cars, country club membership, and a shift from a palatial house to a small apartment. Their resources were almost exhausted, and what broke the camel's back was the ill-fated news that Rishi had been laid off because the agency lost one of its biggest accounts to a competitor. Rishi had been part of the team that was handling that account, so when the top management of our agency decided it was time for heads to roll, Rishi got caught in the storm, even though his supervisor survived.

Despite six months of job hunting, Rishi was

unsuccessful in getting a suitable job. He could not see any light at the end of the tunnel, except a single motivating factor—me, now living in Mumbai."

Her voice was rough with hurt, and I could see the pain in her expressive eyes.

"Rishi had to start fresh. Armed with a belief that he had to rise again, if only for the sake of love, he borrowed $3,000 from me to start a PR agency. He used a significant portion of that money to buy a laptop and rent a small office. He had only three weeks to find a client, for the rest of the money would only last that long. For the next two weeks he zealously tried to win over clients from his former employer's agency, but in vain.

Rishi only had a week's worth of capital left in his pocket. During those two weeks, I had encouraged him, promising unflinching support. We shared a very strong bond, and that triggered him to make a last-ditch attempt at his former employer's agency with a new proposal to save the agency money. Rishi met his former boss and said that it would be cost-effective for the agency to outsource the writing of their media releases to him. It would relieve employees from having to spend hours on routine news dissemination, freeing them to handle more important work for clients.

Two days later he was informed by his ex-boss that his proposal for outsourcing press releases had been accepted by the agency, and he could begin his first assignment the next day. This news was a victory for both him and our love. I had always told him to believe in himself and the Almighty, knowing that the worst would end soon."

"So you told him never to give up?" I asked.

"Yes, that is a credo I live by. With just three days of money left, that good news was the turning point for Rishi's eighteen-day-old one-man start-up PR agency. He never had to look back. His roster of clients grew every quarter, and within fifteen months he had set up four offices across India. The strength of our love had produced a great miracle.

I wanted to go to graduate school to acquire cutting-edge PR and communications skills, but I had postponed the decision until I was certain Rishi was back on his feet. His meteoric rise was reassuring, and that made my decision to apply to a top graduate school in the US easy. We made plans to get married after I got my degree."

"Spectacular success ahead of time can weaken intimate relationships," I interjected.

"Absolutely right. I started to witness a distinct change in Rishi's conduct. He was becoming distastefully narcissistic, and every conversation and leisure activity, including our future plans, had to revolve around him. All along he had known about my grad school plans and had supported my decision. However, that was changing since dramatic success and luck had smiled on him. Given his rising fortune, he felt there was no need for me to study further or continue with a career. Everything he uttered was about him."

"You supported him when the chips were down, but he did not back your decision," I said. "Things must have gone from bad to worse."

"Yes, much worse. He hit me a few times, left me bruised. Whenever I opposed him, he wanted to subjugate me sexually to teach me a lesson. I did not allow him to do so. Instead, I walked out of his life and moved to the United States to start fresh."

"It had become a power game for him," I said, shaking my head. "You must have been devastated."

"Traumatized is an understatement," Meher replied, trying hard to hold back her tears.

"I am sorry to hear about your disturbing past."

She brushed some errant tears away. "The remarkable memories of good times with Rishi were not easy to forget."

"I can well understand. You are a brave woman."

"Thank you."

"What do you think triggered the change in Rishi's behavior?"

"Swift and uncommon growth in terms of money and fame," Meher answered.

"But you said he came from an affluent family," I said, mystified.

"Rishi experienced a double blow, perhaps the most horrible jolt of his life when his father lost his riches and he too was out of work. Rishi's friends and business associates abandoned him. Rejection led to distaste and created a spirit of unimaginable aggression and negativity directed against the upper crust.

Pushed to his limits, Rishi became an entrepreneur with the sole aim of rising from the dungeons of despair, achieving the impossible, and denigrating those who had deserted him when he needed them the most."

"Unfortunately, you, his backbone, became the victim of his arrogance," I said.

"Yes, you are dead right. He thought he knew it all and started to become a control freak. I started to feel claustrophobic and resisted. The rest is painful history."

"Relationships are like a balance sheet that includes assets and liabilities. If there are more liabilities than assets, it hurts. Sometimes badly."

"Yes, the balance sheet of Rishi's and my relationship had some liabilities that I have wiped from my consciousness. However, the liability of abuse still occupies my mind and heart."

"It is not easy to forget a heartache, which may have indelibly scarred your spirit. But it is important for you to do so, or else the ramifications will take a toll on your health and appearance."

"I want to erase the wound. I've tried in different ways but have not succeeded."

"Meher, you are attractive, smart, and talented. You've succeeded in two different countries. You have a lot going for you."

"Ever since Rishi, every single guy I have dated hasn't worked out very well, to say the least. I haven't been able to trust completely."

"Well, it's natural for you to have misgivings about a man's temperament. What happened was deplorable, but do you think it is a good idea to stay wounded?"

"Okay then," Meher said. "A penny for your thoughts?"

"Spoken like an idiomatic communications professional," I chuckled.

"I can be a good listener too, particularly when you have to convince your first *holistic young* client to move on. Let your discourse begin."

"I will make an exception for the lovely Indian lady. You do not have to pay me a fee."

"You're not a good entrepreneur. You buy me dinner, listen to my sob story, and offer to heal my wound for free."

"I'm doing this for a friend and I do not make money off my friends," I replied, extending my hand as a token of friendship.

Meher's eyes met mine with an intense look. She shut her eyes and clasped my hand, saying, "Thank you from the bottom of my heart. You are so nice. God bless you."

We released hands, and I sat back, preparing my response. "When we are tormented through no fault of our own, we begin to own the ordeal. We internalize the trauma and live with repressed emotions. This turns us into suppressed, angry, and touchy individuals. And over a period, it affects our relationships and health. If we do not place trust in our relationships, it won't be long before we hit roadblocks. We start inflicting injury on our loved ones, meting out what we've received. The resentment and shadow of the past then eclipses the present."

Meher nodded. "You make a lot of sense."

"And if that is not enough, injuries of the past can lead to a major ailment or terminal illness. So for the sake of our own happiness and our future, it is important to let bygones be bygones, profit from the disastrous experiences of the past, and give life another chance. History is not always doomed to repeat itself."

"In essence, I need to embrace life and all the love it has to offer."

"Well said," I replied. "Even I could not have expressed it so beautifully."

"You've succinctly assuaged my angst. I promise to work on your advice to get over my painful past. Thank you very much for being there for me."

"You are welcome, but only if you say so as a friend," I quipped.

"I couldn't have expected to find a friend in a

client, and yet you made it possible. You are a wise man. I wish I had met you earlier."

"I have found a friend in a consultant, and you a friend in a client. Everything happens for a reason. We meet many, but become friends with few. The science of friendship is enigmatic and fascinating. We travel or move to another country and form our deepest connection in a distant land." In my mind, I was drawing an intriguing parallel between Meher's move to the United States and my momentous trip to Lima.

"Are you selective about your friends?" Meher asked.

"Yes, I am. I am friendly with all, but friendship is something else. Friends are one of the most precious possessions of my life, so I choose carefully."

"So how do you know who will be allowed entry into your exclusive friendship club?"

"Individuals who have an opinion yet are not judgmental; who are rich, famous, or successful and yet modest; who have little but have not stopped chasing their dreams; who have experienced pain and yet can laugh at themselves; who stand by you in good and bad times; who can motivate when all seems lost; who have lost much and yet have the courage to bounce back; who are continually learning and changing; and who live life to the fullest, even as they honor the responsibilities that come with it."

"And who will find it difficult to become a part of your inner coterie?"

"I avoid befriending negative and pessimistic people. They are the first to restrict your options and criticize genuine efforts."

"What about those whose disposition reeks of superiority or arrogance?"

"I maintain an arm's length from such folks."

"So if I exhibited one or some of these steer-clear-of attributes, would I cease to be your friend?" Meher asked in jest.

"You are a smart woman and will know."

"Sometimes you meet a stranger and feel you have known him for life. Mike, I feel that way about you."

I smiled and expressed my gratitude, although I did not tell her that I felt the same about her. As a relationship coach, you need to have a friendly demeanor with your clients, but you also have to be a thorough professional and keep your emotions in check.

"Have you been told that you are a calming influence?" she asked.

"Now you're stroking my ego."

"I'm just speaking the absolute truth. I feel so comfortable with you. This evening will always be special for me. You've alleviated the hurt I've carried for years."

"Well, you do not have to thank me. You have to

thank yourself for being open to my suggestions," I replied, appreciating Meher's rapid endeavor to get over her excruciating past.

"Now please do me a favor, will you. Let me pick the tab."

I could not say no. It was a wonderful evening, and I was truly pleased with myself.

There was a noticeable change in my counsel of Meher. The lessons of Lima had started showing up. What had made the difference was my heightened sense of self-belief and carrying out Dorothy's lingering words: "Live as if today is your last day. Wear this on your sleeve each day. You will then become the best friend, the favorite supervisor, the unrivaled sweetheart, the wisest adviser, and the greatest listener."

As friends, Meher and I hugged each other goodbye, knowing very well that we needed each other in a crucial phase of our lives. I required Meher's public relations expertise to keep my promise with Dorothy and Andrew, Meher needed me to conquer the demons of her past.

A few minutes later, I received a text message from Meher. *Thank you for showing me the way to unshackle my chains. You are the best. Hugs and Hugs.*

Her text brought a tear to my eyes. It was a drop of glee.

I texted back, *The voice of your text message brings me immense happiness. I send you hugs and smiles. God bless you.* My tears were falling freely. I was unable to control my emotions any longer. Each time an agonizing soul starts to smile, I experience an incomprehensible fulfillment. Something told me then that Meher too must be in tears.

Seconds later, she called. I could hear her weeping. Had I become a clairvoyant? I had sensed a few seconds ago that she must be crying. It was important for her to release her grief. I did not say a word. In her outburst lay her emancipation. She would now be free to love and trust implicitly.

Finally, she spoke. "Thank you for being a true friend. I feel I am born again."

Destiny had put me through my first test sooner than I had envisaged… and I think I had made the grade.

Eight

Over the next two weeks, Meher aggressively pitched my profile with the media. She had adroitly managed to break the Great Wall between our friendship and her profession, and she exceeded the limits of our contract in terms of the time and effort she put into the assignment. It was obvious that my success had become very important to her, and I assumed she was trying to reciprocate the support she had received from me. The day finally came when her arduous efforts bore fruit. I got a call from Sara Jones, a reporter for a well-known newspaper, with a request for a telephone interview. She was of the opinion that my work and book could make for an interesting story, and had a few pertinent questions to ask.

We discussed her queries for half an hour. Sara ended the phone conversation by saying she might call again if necessary.

Barely had I hung up with Sara when I received a call from Tom Barnes, the host of a popular TV show. Meher's persuasive timing could not have been better. Tom was doing a series on members of Generation X who had transitioned from a traditional occupation to an unconventional career. He wanted to know a little about my life story to ascertain if it would make for an interesting inclusion in the series. He had read my book, thanks to Meher's insistence, and found it remarkable.

I gave him a chronicle of my professional transitions and my raison d'être. Tom liked what I recounted and invited me over to the TV station. He wanted to record the interview. Meher deserved a big hug, Andrew a pat on his shoulder, and Dorothy a kiss. The walk to the garden of eminence had begun.

The exhilaration of being on TV to relive my colorful journey of different careers, focusing on the valleys and peaks of my endeavors and which would be watched by viewers across the world, could only be matched with the elation I had experienced as an author. Holding the first copy of my book in my hands had to be akin to a mother's joy of holding her newborn for the first time. I did not have butterflies in my stomach, because I knew if I messed it up, I would lose the opportunity of a lifetime. The lion was waiting to stride out and address the world. Meher coordinated with Tom on the date and time of the shoot, including the dress code, the specific interview questions, and other aspects.

The advantage of hiring a **PR** agency for publicity efforts is well-known, but having a dear friend doubling as my **PR** czarina, putting her might and soul into the assignment, was like igniting a fire that cannot be put out. I was about to be reborn with a **PR** spoon in my mouth.

The drive to the TV station took ten minutes more than I had planned. The tall glass building housed one of America's most famous broadcast companies. I hurried to the elevator, which took me to the second floor within seconds. At the reception desk, a pleasant woman greeted me. I informed her of my appointment with Tom Barnes. Within minutes, Tom entered the reception area and asked me to accompany him to his office.

He led me down a hall, and to our right, behind glass I could see the TV newsroom with lots of computers, flat screen TVs, audio and video equipment, as well as members of the research and production staff, all of them working zealously to provide relevant news and information. When I was in graduate school, I had visited some of the biggest TV stations in the country, so the scene was familiar to me.

A live broadcast was being filmed, and I could see one of the best-known news anchors talking to the cameras. Millions of viewers across the world would be tuned in. Even on the other side of the glass, I could sense the copious energy and stress in the newsroom as updated information kept flowing into it. The news media business is very competitive, and a peek into the world of breaking news, sound bites, and airtime affirmed my belief that behind the perceived glamour of electronic journalism was a lot of sweat and drudgery.

In his office, Tom gave me some hints of how to make my interview memorable. "Take pleasure in being on TV to talk about your purpose and your journey of transition from conventional work to unconventional endeavors. You're not here to be interviewed so much as to have a conversation, so during the recording, please don't take yourself too seriously. As a relationship coach, you know how to charm and convince. Befriend the camera just as you would a prospective client. Don't let any conceptions of what the world might think of you affect what you say in front of the camera."

The time to set the world on fire had arrived. I accompanied Tom to the studio where our interview would be filmed. A small microphone was clipped onto my shirt to pick up my voice easily. Tom smiled at me and signaled a thumbs-up. The camera was ready to roll, and I was on the verge of starting a new chapter of my life. Seconds later, Tom initiated me into the show with a generous introduction.

"The relationship coach who has improved the quality of relationships of many young people across our country, Michael Elliott, it is a pleasure having you on the show."

I smiled at Tom as the camera turned toward me and said, "Thank you."

"Michael is the author of the book *Relationships—24/7*. At the core of the book is the belief that meaningful relationships are based on mutual consideration and open-minded communications. The book caught the imagination of young professionals, and it has turned Michael into a relationship coach for the holistic young, whom he describes as an educated, confident, assertive, and ambitious cohort that enjoys reading and social media, smart phones, tablets, and e-readers.

Michael, you've donned a number of diverse roles. Reporter, consultant, writer, author, and now a relationship coach. What made you adopt such contrasting roles? Was it a penchant to experiment or a longing to make a difference?" Tom asked.

"I'm a hostage of compulsive change who has lived in six cities within the United States and overseas. My father worked as a banker and moved jobs regularly between different cities, and my mother, siblings, and I moved with him, as most families do. Sometime during my childhood, dramatic moves and changes fostered in me a proclivity for the unknown, new, and emerging. The idea of staying in a comfort zone was alien for me. As a logical corollary, my predilection for experimentation and the pursuit of different objectives that also make a noticeable contribution to society a way of life."

"Have some of these transitions been fraught with challenges? What's the difference between being a business reporter and a relationship coach?"

"Life as a business reporter was like a circulating library of high blood pressure. Deadlines and bylines were the outline of my life. Life as a relationship coach is like a circulating library of noteworthy stories and invigorating lessons. As a business journalist, I was exposed to conglomerates and their colossal profits. As a relationship coach, I am exposed to disparate people and their baggage of knotty conundrums. This is where I truly belong."

"What is that one piece of advice you would like share with the holistic young that would make for happier personal relationships?"

Tom had posed the question I was eagerly waiting for. This was the tipping point of the interview, as it would enable me to publicize Dorothy's sagacious advice.

"The mantras for a happy relationship," I answered. "That is, adopt similar interests, condone faults, accept different temperaments, provide room to experiment and space to evolve, and most importantly, develop the ability to have long conversations."

"For the young, do you have any suggestions to enhance their professional development and quality of relationships?"

"Ask for help, even if you are smart or capable, and befriend people who are achievers, believers, and positive-minded strugglers, even if they have failed repeatedly. Stay away from the pessimistic, the disparager, and the skeptic." I was pleased that I was responding with the poise of a seasoned guest on a TV show.

"Do you think the tone of voice can mar the best of relationships?" Tom asked, raising a pertinent point.

"Time and again, the best relationships are marred not because of the actual words used, but because the tone was harsh or rude. Some excellent suggestions or ideas are not accepted merely because of the tone in which they were conveyed. The impolite tongue used as a sarcastic weapon creates a permanent wound, whereas the genteel voice as a positive force reaches the heart and soul of the listener. Relationships that are laced with acerbic words are like ships destined to be wrecked."

"Can you elaborate on the role generosity plays in strengthening personal relations?"

"That is a very good question. Generosity of heterogeneous kind is needed in relationships. To start off, you ought to be lavish in your praise and hearty in appreciation of others. This can be enhanced with acts of compassion, unasked-for favors or gifts, and the ability to forgive. Generosity as a craft of benevolence would most definitely carve a special place in the recipient's heart."

"In a rapidly changing, fast-paced, and short-attention-span world, what is one thing a young person should learn in order to facilitate happier relationships?"

"What I am going to suggest may sound passé, but it's as true for the success of any venture as it is for a younger person to develop strong relationships. Learn to self-reflect. Observe your thoughts, actions, and motives, and you will avoid a plethora of blunders that have marred countless personal lives and professional careers. Self-reflection prepares you to face all kinds of people and state of affairs."

For the next twenty minutes, Tom dug deeper into the hypothetical lives of the younger generation and posed some significant questions relating to personal and professional relationships, and encompassing tomorrow's socio-economic, cultural, and technological changes. After all, young people were inheriting a world where personal relationships were being questioned; existing business models were not providing significant results; a legacy of environmental degradation was endangering the ecosystem; ubiquitous technology was altering social and cultural behaviors; and a person could achieve phenomenal success at a young age, no longer needing to work for thirty years or more to make a difference or become a billionaire. The logical consequence was that the younger generations needed to gear up for a world of immense pressure, in which they would need to make quick decisions about more complex issues in uncertain, rapidly evolving, and competitive conditions. This would drastically alter the dynamics of their relationships with family, friends, and coworkers.

"Time just flew by," Tom said at the end of the interview. "I didn't even realize it. You were terrific."

"Thank you for inviting me onto your show," I said, "and for the tremendous opportunity to get my thoughts across to millions of viewers across the United States and overseas."

Oddly enough, what had mattered most at the beginning of the interview—Tom's approval and the viewers' wholehearted acceptance of my sugges-tions for strong relationships—did not count for me by the end. I had spoken honestly and true to my belief. Such was the power of my candor that I had ceased to look for any external approbation. I left the TV station with a sense of fulfillment.

It takes two to tango, and that is precisely what happened over the next two weeks. First, Sara Jones wrote a feature story about me titled "The Czar of Young Relationships." A few days after that published in her newspaper, my interview with Tom Barnes appeared on TV.

I could not have asked for a better opening to the PR campaign executed by Meher. The duo—Sara's story and Tom's interview—created the Midas touch that led to innumerable e-mails and calls from young people across the country to sign up for my relationship-coaching service. The PR buzz was sustained by various media groups that represented the big and the small of print, broadcast, and online news.

Meher had made sure that every bit of publicity that appeared in any form of the media would subsequently generate more coverage, because we both knew that it was the media that would make me prominent, thereby aiding me in reaching my goal of enhancing the happiness index of the holistic young, leading to a happier and more prosperous nation.

The winds of favor were blowing my way. My roster of clients was swelling. Due to this sudden growth in business, I was required to expand my office space in Lincoln Park and hire additional office staff. My book hit the best-seller list. Invitations to speak at universities, seminars, and related events followed, and through the next year I traveled across North America coaching, speaking, and signing, as well as continuing to meet clients in my office.

I discovered the mindset of the North American youth through their eyes, voices, expressions, and silence. They were eager to create their own paradigms and follow the paths they had envisioned for themselves. I had answers to most of their queries or concerns, yet I found myself at a loss with some tough questions or situations that I was asked to comment on. I was honest enough to admit that I did not have all answers, although I did my best to come up with an explanation or a solution. It was important to retain the personal touch. I made sure that as far as possible, I replied to each e-mail and message I received, and I stayed accessible to my existing clients and the media.

My rise was unusually rapid, yet providence continued to be extremely gracious with me. Eighteen months into the client and media blitz, I signed a two-million-dollar book deal with a major publisher in New York to write the story of my life.

While I was mighty pleased that my second book had resulted in such a healthy contract even before its birth, and that it would certainly make its presence felt thanks to it being backed by a renowned publisher, I was on the horns of a dilemma. What was I going to say? I knew only one thing for sure— I would dedicate the book to the young people who I hoped would generate historic changes in an increasingly collaborative and wired world.

My life was a colorful amalgam of unusual experiences, continual change, and intimate relationships with some of the most fascinating and wise people that graced our world. Should I collate my thoughts around the aforementioned occurrences and bring out discerning aspects to strengthen personal and professional relationships of the holistic young? My quandary did not last long thanks to Meher, for I knew I could rely on her to provide an outline for the contracted book.

Meher was no longer just a PR specialist, media adviser, or friend. She had become a confidante, and between us we had shared some of the deepest secrets of our lives. By then my sixth sense told me that Meher loved me, yet she held herself back because she knew I would never fall in love with her. She knew about Dorothy and how strongly I felt about her. I never told Meher, but if I hadn't been in love with Dorothy, I might have started dating Meher. Even amidst my spectacular rise, hours of coaching and speaking sessions, once a week we would engage in long and meaningful conversation over coffee or a meal.

We had one such meaningful discussion over lunch at Panera Bread in Evanston. Meher ordered her favorite—Greek salad, while I decided to get the pasta primavera. As we ate our meals, I said, "Meher, what I find intriguing is the theory of reincarnation. I've read about it. Can you tell me what you know about it?"

"Before that, let me ask you a question. Why is it that young kids take so easily and effortlessly to laptops, tablets, video games, and smart phones? How do we identify a child prodigy?"

"To answer your first question, it's because they're born into a world that is swamped with computers, video games, and smart phones. To answer the second one, a child prodigy exudes certain characteristics or talent for a particular vocation, be it sports, the arts, science, or writing. These inborn traits are tapped early, which is why the child became a phenomenon."

Meher nodded in agreement. "So let me elucidate further with an example, which please take note of with an open mind. He who died in December 2002 was possibly reborn in January 2003. Before he passed away in 2002, he was already exposed to computers, the Internet, cell phones, video games, and our rapidly changing world. In his new incarnation, he would carry forward from his previous life his knowledge, temperament, and skills, which may explain why a young kid takes so naturally to electronic gizmos, gadgets, and technology. As regards the second answer, I couldn't agree with you more. If a kid exudes a special innate talent, and a parent or an elder is able to identify it early on, the possibility of a child prodigy emerging in the family enhances. Whether the parent was in the know or not, the knowledge from the kid's past life was tapped and developed to create a child sensation."

"Fascinating thought. I'll have to delve more into the reincarnation theory," I replied.

"There is a deep connection between the reincarnation theory and spirituality. Mike, you are a spiritual person, even though you may not be aware of it. If I were you, I would try to acquire more spiritual knowledge," Meher said.

I could not help but draw a parallel between Dorothy's first meeting with Andrew and my first reincarnation-spirituality conversation with Meher. By the end of Dorothy and Andrew's first rendezvous in Chicago, their roles had reversed. Dorothy had spoken as the communications expert and Andrew had looked like a novice. In Evanston, Meher appeared to be the life and relationship specialist and me a rookie.

"What makes you an ardent advocate of spirituality?" I asked.

"That is a long story. It will bore you," Meher replied candidly.

I was not in a mood to give up. After all, that was the nature of my job. I could get Meher to reveal her spirituality faith story, without sounding personal or probing.

"I am a good listener and I have all the time. You can talk for as long as you like," I responded.

"If you insist… Let me tell you a true story. You can draw your conclusions from that."

She proceeded to describe her spiritual tale. "A senior executive in an international airline company was the cynosure of all eyes in the airline industry because of his leadership skills and meteoric rise. While he believed in the Almighty, what was slowly going to his head was the collective exuberance of his professional success, a loving wife, successful off-spring, and a flamboyant lifestyle. At the back of his mind, the thought began to germinate that he was the sole doer, and that his unusual success was due to his brilliance and well-planned moves.

He had it all and began to feel that this would always last. But destiny thought otherwise. Unexpectedly, one day his wife breathed her last within fifteen minutes of complaining about chest pain. His support system and emotional strength came from his doting wife who was barely fifty-eight years old. Her untimely demise meant that his world had come to an end. He lost interest in his job, and this lion of a leader turned as docile as a housecat.

From then on, his nights also began to go down-hill. Almost each night, he would fondly remember his wife and weep for hours in his bed. Despite the outpouring of love and care he received so gener-ously from his children and their families, he was a broken man. This went on for fifteen months. As if this were not enough, another tragedy occurred. His son-in-law, who was the managing director of a prestigious organization in India and had gone away to New Zealand for a business conference, out of the blue suffered a brain hemorrhage and had to be rushed to the hospital for medical care. The son-in-law did not survive, and when the father-in-law got the news, he was devastated. The heavens had fallen on him. His son-in-law was as dear to him as his two sons, and together they had many cherished memories.

For the next decade, the retired airline manager tried to move on in life. He kept himself occupied with voluntary and community service, and also enjoyed watching his grandchildren grow up in front of his eyes. This made him smile once again on the outside. But deep inside his heart, he lived with the pain of separation and never truly recovered from these untimely tragedies. This was not the last of the bereavements, though. One evening the telephone rang, and his youngest son answered. When he put the phone down, tears started rolling down from his cheeks, and he broke the news of his elder brother's death from a heart attack.

The departure of the eldest son made the elderly gentleman nearly drown in grief. However, thanks to the efforts of his youngest son and daughter-in-law, who cajoled him to move away from ritualistic remembrance of God toward self-actualization and spirituality, he was able to experience serenity, happiness, and detachment in the last few years of his life.

He once said to his youngest son and daughter-in-law, 'The revival in my spirits is only because of the Almighty's grace and your support, but each tragedy which engulfed me was my own doing because I was never mentally prepared for the inevitable truth that whatever good comes our way is only for a short period, and is as slippery as soap. The consequences of grief overtook my happy memories, and I wasted my life thereafter. If I had been spiritually inclined through my formative years, these tragedies would not have been averted because they were a part of my destiny, but I would have absorbed them with palpable peace and accepted them as the cardinal truth of life."

Meher paused for a breather and then declared, "The retired senior airline executive was my grandfather, and his youngest son and daughter-in-law are my parents."

I was speechless. Nevertheless, I felt that Meher had more to say. I pushed my bottle of water toward her. She took a few sips and then articulated a thought-provoking imperative.

"We as humans have predictable wants, attitudes, feelings, and needs. People are richer today, but their inner selves remain undeveloped, self-centered, gnarled, and filled with misgivings toward life, and that leads to discordant relationships. The holistic development and happiness quotient of a country would thrive best in the garden of spirituality. After all, spiritual awakening leads to happier relationships.

Just as young people are introduced to the importance of education and career planning, they ought to be introduced to the process of self-discovery through spiritualism. The school of spiritualism—the most unique and potent school in a person's life prepares us for the good and the bad times and the dynamically changing nature of relationships."

"Meher, your spiritual story is soul stirring and profound. How do you know so much? Do you have a spiritual guru?"

"Thank you. Yes, I do have a spiritual guru, and whatever I know is because of my master who is an embodiment of wisdom and grace," Meher replied as an unswerving disciple. The very mention of her guru brought a sparkle to her eyes.

"You are a loyal follower, and I understand the significance of the presence of a spiritual guide in an individual's life. However, I have a serious question that baffles me. When God or true apostles of love, peace, and happiness have never charged a fee or accepted money from their disciples or devotees for their sermons, benevolence, or acts of compassion, is it fair for most modern spiritual gurus to levy a fee or accept offerings from their disciples? When coffers are full of gifts and donations from credulous followers, and marketing, merchandizing, and public relations strategies are used to create spiritual leaders, doesn't spirituality then become an organized business?" This was a question that had befuddled me for years.

"Well, my guru does not advertise to amass disciples or charge a fee for sermons. They do not accept any donations or gifts. They do not want anything from a devotee. You make a very valid point, and I couldn't agree with you more. To my mind a true spiritual guru ought not to accept any material gifts for the love, compassion, and revelation bestowed by them on their disciples or followers.

"In my opinion, the quest for a true master or guru starts and ends with a simple test: Does he or she offer their teachings for free and without requesting their disciples' monetary involvement or commitment via gifts, publicity, donation, and fees? If yes, then follow the guru, for the true spiritual master only gives and never accepts anything in kind or cash."

Meher's words highlighted a noteworthy point that would abet the search for an uncommon yet true guru.

"Well, you are lucky to have found a true master. It sure is rare to find one these days," I answered.

Meher's cogent explanation made our conversation one of the most memorable discussions of our association. She had imparted a unique perspective about the higher order of life and relationships.

*

This, however, did not help me with figuring out what to write in my book. Meher suggested something that at the outset did not sit well with me. That I should write a novel about a relationship coach who inadvertently becomes the inheritor of a legacy, thanks to the journey of a lifetime and an extraordinary woman. That would make for an interesting read as opposed to a nonfiction book filled with the usual obscurity to prominence story. I disagreed with her, only because I knew a novel would require me to write about certain events of my life that hitherto had remained very personal.

Given the atypical story of my life, though, a piece of fiction would certainly make for better reading and spruce up sales, but it would also reveal Dorothy. She was a very private person; so how could I expose her to the world? How could I betray her trust? I had no problem in recreating Andrew's character. However, writing in the public domain about Dorothy was unacceptable to me.

I could change her identity and name, yet once the novel was published, it would call for media scrutiny and a lot of questions. I wasn't afraid of answering questions, but I had to respect Dorothy's privacy.

We deliberated hard, argued long, and thankfully found the way out through our animated discussions. The protagonist of the novel would be the heir of the legacy of an eminent relationship coach, but there would be no mention of a fascinating lady's immense contribution in shaping the destiny of the central character. I would use my imagination to modify my life story, names, identities, and situations, and yet write an engaging piece of fiction that would hopefully make the reader think, dream, laugh, or cry.

I had a year to complete my manuscript, and given that this would be a lot of work and the most ambitious writing project of my life, I had to develop a plan that would give priority to writing each day and yet strike a fine balance between coaching and speaking sessions.

For the next four months, from Monday through Friday, I woke up at five and wrote diligently for four hours, with a five or ten minute break every forty-five minutes. The rest of the day I devoted to clients or promotional activities. Late-night indulgences were confined to Friday or Saturday nights. I did not make any exceptions on a weekday, even for Meher.

What impressed Meher the most was not the two million dollars riding on the success of my book, but the discipline with which I pursued the project without comprising on my coaching and speaking commitments. I wanted to better the timeline and complete the manuscript within six months to allow enough time for edits and rewriting.

At the beginning of the fifth month, I stepped it up and wrote six hours a day, including weekends. And yet each weekend, I made it a point to have an evening meal with Meher. The only difference from before was that we would have an early dinner followed by coffee or a quick drink. I was careful not to have more than one small glass of Scotch so that I would be back home in time to get adequate sleep for an early start the following morning. And finally the day dawned when I had completed the first draft of the manuscript. I even had a title for it—*The Suitable Inheritor.*

Meher read through the draft and gave her candid, constructive opinion. Once again she and I differed; however, this time it was about the dedication page. I had dedicated the book to young people across the world, while she felt it ought to be dedicated to Dorothy and Andrew. I had paid a glowing tribute to Andrew in the acknowledgments section and stayed away from mentioning the name or contribution of Dorothy. It wasn't ingratitude, and Meher and I both knew this very well. Dorothy Porter, as former editor of *People Mantra*, was well-known, and consequently it was plausible that I had benefited from Dorothy's guidance. Meher thought this was both a fitting way to incorporate Dorothy's name, and that it wouldn't arouse any intrusive questions from readers or the media. Meher had a pertinent point, yet I was not completely convinced. Perhaps, I thought, I should speak with Andrew, because nobody else could understand my predicament as well as he.

Ever since my momentous journey to Lima, Andrew and I had spoken to each other only twice. He was constantly in my thoughts, yet I did not want to disturb an ailing man. A call to check on his health was due, and if he sounded good, I could get his opinion on Meher's suggestion.

A day later, I called Andrew in Lima. His father Martin answered the phone, and what I heard next was as painful as an arrow that pierces the heart. Andrew had died a week earlier. Martin knew of me because Andrew had left with him a small note for me, written a few days before he passed away. It was as if Andrew knew he was about to move on, and even in his frail health he wanted to leave something for his protégé. The subsequent torrent of tears that surged from my eyes summarized my inconsolable pain. I felt as if I had lost everything. I could not talk and regrettably hung up on Martin. How could I express my condolences and assuage his grief when I was utterly devastated? That day I did not take any calls or reply to any messages or e-mails. I don't know when I stopped crying and crawled into bed.

Next morning, I woke up feeling low and empty. Andrew had left a void that only time could fill. I knew I had to apologize to his father for hanging up on him. I used my landline to call him. Martin was gracious enough to overlook the rudeness. What followed was a heart-to-heart chat about Andrew, the son, the friend, the coach, and the mentor. During the course of the conversation, I decided that I would follow Meher's suggestion. Martin was pleased to know that my second book would be dedicated to Andrew. I asked him if he wanted me to travel to Lima to spend some time with him or if he wished he could visit me in Chicago. Martin was a brave man and said he was doing fine.

I requested him to read Andrew's final note over the phone, which he politely declined. Instead he asked me for my address and promised it would be at my doorstep very soon. Andrew had sealed the note in an envelope with my name and phone number on it, and then had given it to Martin to be sent to me. The contents of the note were personal and meant only for my eyes, and Martin wanted to respect the wishes of his deceased son.

Once I got off the phone, I noticed I had five voice-mail messages. Meher had been frantically trying to reach me since the morning as a senior editor of a prominent British magazine wanted to write a feature article on my meteoric rise as a relationship coach. This was a huge opportunity to reach out to the young people of the UK, and also garner pre-launch publicity in Great Britain for my forthcoming novel. Great Britain is traditionally among the world's leading English book markets. I was in no mood to give any interviews, and for once I ignored Meher's messages. When her attempts to get hold of me on my phone did not bear fruit, she texted me. I disregarded those messages too.

My silence was unusually odd and the cause of uneasy concern at her end. Since we had met, I had never behaved so strangely. I was known for my quick responses to phone calls and messages. So when she showed up at my door later in the evening, I was not surprised. One look at my sullen face and she knew something was amiss. She did not say anything, yet her caring eyes told me she wanted to help. At that moment I could not hold my tears back, and I told her of Andrew's death. Next thing I knew, she was hugging me tight to console me.

That evening, if there was one person from whom I wanted a big and consoling hug, it was Dorothy. I knew Meher was not Dorothy, but there was something compassionately kindhearted about Meher's hug that made me stay nestled against her warm shoulders. During moments of anguish or grief, there is something divine about a woman's sympathetic embrace. It is extremely comforting and can assuage pain without a word being exchanged.

As we held tightly, we could feel each other breathing. We looked intently at each other. Our bodies were in a state of mutual attraction.

I could sense Meher wanted me to make the first move. I was overwhelmingly attracted to her, yet Dorothy was still a presence in my life. I loved Dorothy more than this sort of temporary allure. Meher had always gone the extra mile for me, and if I took advantage of the situation that night with no concern for the day after, it would be grossly unfair to her. I hugged her tightly; thanked her for offering her shoulder to lean on; and, as embarrassed as I was, stepped back awkwardly. Meher did not bat an eyelid, even as she continued to stare at me. I was ill at ease and did not know which way to look.

Ten seconds later, she said, "Mike, you really are madly and earnestly in love with Dorothy. Few men would have been able to resist me after getting so close to me."

"I am sorry, Meher, if I've hurt you. You are truly a very beautiful woman, but I cannot love you the way I love Dorothy. Please don't ask me why, because I won't be able to put it in plain words. The writer in me will fail to give an explanation of matters of the heart. I hope you will forgive me."

"You don't have to say sorry. I understand. Dorothy is a lucky woman. In fact, I am envious of her. She has found a man who loves her so dearly, he will not even succumb in a moment of weakness to another woman. I wish the world had more guys like you, Mike."

Meher was putting on a brave and magnanimous front, even though she and I both knew I had hurt her.

"Thank you," I said. "You have a very special place in my life, and don't ever forget that."

She smiled and nodded, and then digressed to talk about scheduling time for the most important interview of my life. I was going to be the cover article for an acclaimed British magazine with worldwide circulation. At the end of our discussion, I told Meher that I had decided to take her advice and dedicate the book to Andrew. I admitted that the news of Andrew's death had solved my predicament.

That evening, I did not want Meher to leave. She could help mitigate the downcast feeling that was overwhelming me. Even though I had a lot of male friends, I was always closer to women. And each time a pall of gloom descended in my life, I found it easier to come out of it if I had a female friend with me. Women by nature are more compassionate than men, and in moments of tragic bereavement, the receptive ears, warm hugs, and supportive shoulders of an empathetic lady are the perfect succor to a sullen heart and mind.

I managed to persuade Meher to stay over for dinner. A glass of wine with pizza makes for unrestrained and interesting conversation. We took a trip down memory lane, revisiting the extraordinary saga of two walls. The first wall—a Great Wall erected to safeguard a client-agency association. The second wall—an intimate and personal wall built to last between a man and a woman who were extremely fond of each other and yet could never become a couple. Some relationships have no name, so we classify them as special friends. These are not soul mates but special mates who laugh and cry with you, who dine and walk with you, who agree and disagree with you, and who share all with you.

I then made a request of Meher that few women might have agreed to. I wanted to lie down with my head on her lap to get some sleep. She assented to my request. As I lay down, she pulled from her bag Kahlil Gibran's enchanting book *The Prophet* and began reading from it. The magical words "Love knows not its own depth until the hour of separation" were fitting for the state of my mind. Andrew had departed for another world and Dorothy had parted ways with me for another sacrifice.

What was it about love and relationships that made them a double-edged sword? The sharp edges of life had pain and pleasure on either side of the relationship blade. No matter how deep and happy a relationship may be, one fine day the pleasure of togetherness would be shattered by the pain of separation. Was the pain of separation more powerful than the joy of special moments? Did death mean the end of a relationship, or did it lead to unparalleled proximity with the spirit of the deceased? Was separation a severance from the old and a chance to welcome the new? Oblivious to Meher who continued to read from *The Prophet*, I was distracted by this plethora of questions. Eventually sensing she was reading to an inattentive mind, Meher looked at me and asked if something was bothering me.

"No, Well, maybe. Well, actually, yes," I said, and then proceeded to disclose my preoccupied musings.

Meher did not offer any explanation, although she might have had the answers. Instead, she gently took my hand and walked me over to the bed in my bedroom and sat down with me, all while holding onto my hand. I noticed her eyes. In those brown eyes, I saw all the love and care that she had for me. I asked her to lie down beside me. She planted a kiss on my temple and whispered, "Try to get some sleep." Something magical happened then. I dozed off almost instantaneously, thanks to Meher's angelic touch. She told me later that she left once she was convinced I was fast asleep.

Two days later I received Andrew's last note. As I tore open the envelope, a lump was rising in my throat as I remembered his last words to me: "I want you to make a promise. You will not let Dorothy's sacrifice go in vain. You will become the most renowned relationship coach the world has ever known."

The short note was handwritten, and that made it even more precious. A dying man had thought of me in his last moments and taken the trouble to put pen to paper. The note read:

Dear Mike,

By the time you get this note, I will have departed this life. You made my last wish possible. Thank you for bringing about the reunion with Dorothy. As she had promised, she visited me a short while ago. We held hands and wept together. A dying man can now rest in peace. I am convinced that you will become the most effective relationship coach the world has ever known. You are indeed a worthy heir.

May God shower the choicest of blessings on you. Thank you for coming to Lima and for being a true friend. Hopefully we will meet in some other world in some other time.

Warm hugs and love,

Andrew

My eyes were moist with gratitude. Andrew was not only an eminent individual, he was also a very big man. He knew only to give, bless, and thank. This was one of the two most valuable letters of my life handwritten by a special person, and I read it not once or twice, but ten times during the course of the day. I was pleased that Dorothy had made it in time to see Andrew again. A moving, gratifying moment for Dorothy and Andrew, and a deeply fulfilling piece of news for me.

The journey to Lima was now complete. Andrew had departed in peace, Dorothy had kept her word, and I had by the grace of God been the instrument that initiated the reunion. I thanked the Lord for his graces.

NINE

The hour-long telephone interview with Margaret Evans, a senior editor of the British magazine, went well. I had found that every interview consisted of both anticipated and unexpected queries. Margaret wanted to know more about my second book and the inspiration behind my meteoric rise as a relationship coach. I provided an outline of the book, focusing on Andrew's providential bestowal and a cursory insight into my life story. Margaret was not convinced. She continued to probe, and also wanted to know how an unmarried man could become such a successful relationship coach. She suggested either I was in love with an extraordinary woman or I had loved and lost.

Unknown to her, the truth was a blend of the duo. I could not disclose the Dorothy narrative to her, yet I had to find a reasonable explanation to answer her question. My believable answer for how

I'd come to understand the nuances of personal and professional challenges and relationships was that I had experienced the rainbow of life in all its forms. I had lived in different cities and towns, in lavish homes and unadorned apartments, studied at the best and the ordinary, walked with the victor and the defeated, dined with the maverick and the conformist, observed the eminent and the subordinate, experimented with mainstream and non-mainstream professions, enjoyed the security of a good job and the spirited risk of entrepreneurship, experienced success and failure, and dated women of different ethnicities. The richness of these diverse experiences had provided me the opportunity to suggest simple strategies to deal with shades of life, complicated relationships, assorted mindsets, and make a small attempt to create a better tomorrow for the younger generations that graced our world.

Margaret accepted my explanation, this summary of the essence of my life, because it was filled with a conviction that was instinctive, effortless, and heartfelt. A month later, the magazine ran a three-page story with my picture on the cover. There could not have been a better international prepublishing buzz for my novel. The website for the London-based magazine had fifteen million unique monthly visitors, most of them from Great Britain, South Africa, Asia-Pacific, and the Middle East. Meher's adroit PR efforts and Margaret's objective yet glowing tribute also led to new client sign-ups from those areas. From my office, I could employ mobile technology to be face-to-face with my overseas clients and work with them to resolve their sticky relationship issues. The world outside the United States had become a smaller place for me.

During this international growth of my coaching practice, I revised my manuscript as requested by my editor.

The publisher of my second book was among the world's leading publishing houses, yet I knew that the marketing of my book was too important to be left only to the publisher. I had to put in place my own publicity plan, and who better than Meher to do so. She suggested we draft separate promotion plans, saying that two heads were better than one—and two wordsmiths were smarter than one. And she was a hard taskmaster, for she also said, "You should come up with at least two new book-promotion ideas that have not been implemented in the past by us. Our time starts now."

She gave us four days to formulate these plans, and during this time we would not meet or even talk on the phone.

When you are fighting the clock, you have to stay calm and focused. As I began writing the publicity plan, I couldn't help but believe that time and destiny were on my side. Nature's plan for fulfillment of the special purpose of my life had manifested itself through Lima, Dorothy, Andrew, and Meher, as well as prominent media personalities. One common thing that had led to my dramatic rise was the entrance of distinct achievers from various professions into my life at different points in time. When I was meant to struggle, otherwise right decisions went wrong, arduous efforts yielded average results, and well-thought plans did not work out as expected. When the aura of positive developments began to surface, extraordinary people had descended into my life to play vital roles in my untypical progression.

After four days—the longest time Meher and I had gone without speaking—we met at my office to go over our respective publicity plans. She was impressed by two promotion ideas I had incorporated into my plan: adapt the novel for a film or TV show and participate in book fairs and festivals. She had two amazing ideas of her own. Appointing young ambassadors to promote the book across the United States and internationally; and a fundraising event, with the proceeds going toward the education of underprivileged children.

Over the next two days, we deliberated and argued over the major, expensive, and innovative promotion ideas that were parts of our respective plans. Eventually we developed a plan that was cost-effective and creative, and integrated book marketing and communications strategies, including advertising and sales tactics. We decided to suggest the publisher cosponsor the full-page ad in the *New York Times* Book Review. We then apprised the publisher of the salient features of our publicity plan. Given our commitment to pull out all the stops to make the novel a best seller, and their belief that it had the makings of a chartbuster, they acceded to our request to share the budget.

Confident that the book would succeed beyond my expectation, I came to believe the novel would be the defining moment of my life, the game-changer that would enable me to keep my promise to be the most renowned relationship coach in the world, and reverently honor Dorothy's sacrifice.

A few months into our marketing plan, *The Suitable Inheritor* was launched in the United States and around the world in both print, digital, and audio versions, available to purchase, download, borrow, or hear across varied mediums—brick and mortar bookstores, libraries, online retailers, e-readers, tablets, and smart phones.

I recorded the audio book with the aid of a creative voice artist, who provided the discriminating input to bring the words, characters, and story to life.

Our integrated marketing plan bettered our expectations. Book reviews—the first test that defines the true calling card of a book—were incredibly positive in domestic and international publications. TV interviews were featured in primetime broadcasts, spurring the visibility and sales of the novel. My book tour to major cities of the United States opened to full houses. The young-ambassadors program, which had enrolled young folks at university campuses and mainstream and non-mainstream professions to publicize and sell copies of the book for commission, yielded mind-blowing sales figures. The fundraising dinner event in New York garnered a significant amount, enough money to fund the college education of at least ten underprivileged children.

My speaking invitations quadrupled. The most gratifying of these were invitations to address the graduating classes of some of the top schools in the country. Reading excerpts from the novel at private book-club gatherings was an amazing experience, and it gave me the opportunity to interact one-on-one with readers and get candid feedback, some of which was constructive criticism. At these book clubs, I met some incredible people who later became friends. Invitations to write articles for well-known magazines and newspapers led to a syndicated column that was carried by several major publications. These publications had an international readership, and that helped my thoughts reach different parts of the world.

The most important of them all, I sent my thank-you notes to the editors and reporters who wrote about my book; the readers who took time out of their busy schedules to write to me; the coordinators of the fundraising event, who had supported a cause very close to my heart; all the people at the publishing house who had been involved with the book for their wholehearted support in this incredible journey; and many others who had contributed in making my book a global best seller.

It was official. I had become the best-known relationship coach for the younger generations. The world now knew of Andrew's contribution to my spectacular rise. Meher also got credit for her dexterous public-relations skills, some even christening her as the foremost book-marketing professional of our times. I couldn't agree more with them, but what they did not know was that behind a remarkable book publicist were a special friend and an incredibly amazing woman who loved me unconditionally.

Dorothy's role, on the other hand, was still cloaked in secrecy.

Caught up in the whirlwind of making *The Suitable Inheritor* an international success, Meher and I got overinvolved with interviews, tours, events, and the like. Much as we wanted to privately celebrate the novel's success, we could not find the time to spend a leisurely evening together. The task of crafting a best seller and the goal of reaching the acme as a relationship coach had been accomplished. It was time to rejoice and party, and what better way than to have an exclusive and quiet party with only two invitees—Meher and I. The venue would be either her home or mine, so that we could talk, laugh, eat, drink, and reminisce as we pleased.

I suggested her apartment, but she took the easy way out. She did not want to have to clean her home and coerced me into hosting the exclusive revelry at my abode. She also specified a dress code for me: no suits, ties, or dress slacks. They were all too boring.

Meher had seen a lot of me in suits and what I considered business-casual attire. Her dress code left me with only one option: jeans with a party shirt. I couldn't insist on a dress code for her since she had already told me she was going to dress to surprise me. I could make an educated guess. She would almost certainly wear a black dress because each time she dressed in black, she looked lovely.

At 8:30 p.m. sharp, I heard my doorbell. I knew who to expect, but I was swept away when I opened the front door. Meher was wearing skintight jeans, a see-through white T-shirt with a camisole underneath, and boots. She looked smoking hot. I had always known she had a good body, but her tight jeans displayed the shapely fullness of her thighs. Her gaze ran up and down my body, making me weak in my knees, and then she greeted me with a warm hug and a peck on my cheek. I was nervous, and she knew it. Before my emotions got out of control, I had to be in charge of them. I invited her in. She walked into the living room, and I followed. We sat down on the couch, and before I could think of what to say, she spoke.

"I am so tired and thirsty. I think I need a glass of wine. Can you please bring my thirsty soul a glass of white wine?"

As a wine lover, I had saved a bottle of fine wine for a special occasion.

After she'd taken a few sips of wine, Meher drew closer to me and whispered into my ear, "Good wine can't be rushed. It must be savored."

The electric current between us got stronger. I could feel the heat radiating off her as she inched closer to me.

I am not a hermit or saint. I'm a man, I thought. Yet I had Dorothy at the back of my mind. I could not betray my love. At the same time, I could not ignore the fact that Meher's unconditional support and adoration had played a significant role in all of my recent successes. An agonizing moral dilemma afflicted my mind and body.

I had known Meher for a few years, and that night I could read her mind like a book. Her romantic gesture to rock my heart was an attempt to give her body the chance to experience the love of a lifetime. She knew I would never choose her for Dorothy, yet she wanted the whole of me to complete the journey of love and togetherness in one night. Her eyes, mischievous demeanor, body language, and skintight jeans were a potent combination

that few men would have been able to resist. Being a
normal man with normal urges, I could succumb to
her sensual magnetism. The truth was, though, that
I was willing to disregard my self-control and will-
power in order to give Meher what she longed for;
and through our union, I would thank her for bringing the accolades of the world at my doorstep. I also
knew that if I made love to Meher, it would be our
secret for life.

"Meher, if you don't mind my saying so, you are
looking smoldering hot," I said.

"Not as hot as you," she replied.

"I don't accept that. Look at you. Only a saint
would not take notice of you."

"What's the point if the man I love pays
no attention?"

"And if the man you love closes his eyes to the
world tonight, would you open up to him?"

"Only if I have the whole of him in mind, body,
and spirit."

"He is certainly very attracted to you, so he may
give himself to you ardently."

"The passion should not ebb. I hope he has staying power."

"Well, he can quench your thirst and yet not
feel extinguished."

"Is that confidence or impudence?"

"You could call it as audacious as your body-
hugging attire."

"Can you describe it?"

"Stunning and sensuous," I said.

"Wouldn't you want to know what the lady thinks of you?"

"I can't wait to hear."

"You want to make a guess."

"Your guess is as good as mine."

"She thinks you are an Adonis," Meher whispered in my ear.

"Thank you. It feels great because the compliment comes from a beautiful woman."

"Mike, is Dorothy as beautiful as me?" Meher dropped a shocker of a question.

I did not want to answer. Comparisons are odious. Yet I replied with all the tact at my command. "Meher, you are lovely and truly a wonder of the world."

"But I cannot take the place of Dorothy, can I?"

"You have no idea how delightfully fascinating you are."

"So what do you find most attractive about me?" she asked.

"Your expressive eyes," I replied.

"But when you opened your door to me, you only seemed to look at my skintight jeans."

"Well, that was because I was in a state of shock. I've never seen you in tight jeans."

"So what was the first thing that came to your mind when you saw me in these tight jeans?"

"You want me to be honest?"

"Yes. The truth and only the truth."

"'Smoking hot' was the first expression on my mind."

"Did you think of making love to me?"

"Yes, I did. I am not a hermit."

"So what stopped you from doing so? Dorothy or me?"

"Both. Dorothy is my soul mate, and you are my special mate. She is my spiritual love, and you are the woman I am exceptionally fond of. I cannot forget her, yet I find it difficult to resist your magnetic pull. Dorothy is my inspiration. You are an exclusive gift who has given her heart and soul to help me in my life's quest. If I kiss you, I betray Dorothy, and if I don't, I hurt you."

"Mike, you don't have to make love with me because I made you famous. You don't owe me anything. You and I are mature enough to know that my efforts would not have yielded anything if you were really not good at what you do."

"Meher, you are an incredibly special woman. I would be the luckiest guy in the whole world if I got intimate with you. But I would never want to play with your feelings or do something that we would regret."

"You know what I like about you, Mike? You are so committed to Dorothy, and you are brutally honest. I love you from the bottom of my heart. I have never loved any man as much as you. I am aware that I cannot ever take the place of Dorothy, but my love for you is so intense, even one night of passionate union of body, mind, and spirit would be enough blissful fervor to last me a lifetime."

In our subconscious minds, we both knew we were going to make love that night because of obvious reasons—an overpowering mutual desire and the depth of our reciprocated adoration, as well as gratitude on my part and her wish to touch the unattainable at least once.

The next thing I knew, our lips had met and we were kissing passionately as if we had longed for this moment forever. Shortly thereafter, we moved to the bedroom. We just could not stop kissing and touching each other. She then climbed on top of me, quickly pinned my hands to the bed, and unbuttoned my shirt.

The rest was, in one word, ethereal. We surrendered our supple bodies to each other. She gave to receive and I gave to thank.

Our lovemaking was interspersed with tender bed talk as we held hands, caressed, and cajoled. That memorable night, Meher undressed me, but she also uncovered her deepest emotions. She poured her heart out to share the most precious and private moments of her life. She was indeed a wonder of the world, and that night I thanked God for bringing the finest special mate into my life.

The touch of joy and the saga of ecstasy carried through the night and well into the morning. As the sun rose, we kissed each other gently. It would be the last time we would kiss. A new day had dawned, but Meher and I would stay the same—special mates who would never stop caring about each other, doting on each other, and arguing with each other. Perhaps we were unique and few would be able to fathom the nature and depth of our association.

TEN

An author and relationship coach had become an air and road warrior. Universities, associations, and corporations across the United States invited me to speak. As part of these speaking tours, I traveled extensively within the country. Participation in domestic and international book fairs and festivals provided me an enormous opportunity to strengthen my connection with readers, meet with potential clients, and speak to the media that covered these festivals.

With each speaking engagement, I added a building block to my learning process. The attendees kept me on my feet with their intriguing inquisitions and thoughts. As is the norm, not all feedback or exchanges were complimentary, thank heavens. An excess of applause veneers the truth and impedes the development of a writer and a coach. The best takeaway from these trips was the constructive disapproval that I received from insightful readers. It would only make me a better writer and relationship coach.

Michael Elliott had finally found his place in the sun and was fulfilling the promise made to Andrew and Dorothy. He now had the world at his feet… yet something felt incomplete.

All along the journey of my ascendancy, I had been aware of a void created by the secret longing to be physically together with Dorothy. Even a relationship coach is human enough to desire touchable closeness.

It is a cliché that behind every successful man is a woman, but behind the extraordinary success of this man was the remarkable sacrifice of an exceptional woman. Her sacrifice was undeniably remarkable—and now that I had realized my dream, the time to reunite with Dorothy had arrived. The time to make a trip to Lima had come.

Meher had read my mind. She did, after all, know me rather well. On a beautiful summer evening at her home she said, "Mike, you are now, as they would say in India, the maharaja of human relationships."

"Thank you, Meher. In Lima, Dorothy and Andrew showed me the way. Here in Chicago, you made it possible. You are a darling. God bless you." I held her left hand for a few seconds to express my deep gratitude to my special mate. From India, the land of spirituality, an angel had come into my life and transformed it forever.

"I haven't told you," she said, "but I found your novel simple yet compelling. There are unforgettable passages in *The Suitable Inheritor* that penetrated my heart and touched me in ways few novels ever have. You have achieved all you set out to do. Now is the time for the relationship czar to court his darling Dorothy once again."

Despite her generous words, I could see the pain of imminent separation in her eyes. She loved me immensely, yet she was ready to let go of me.

"Meher, when I returned from Lima to Chicago, little did I know that I would be so lucky again so soon. I had just met Dorothy, and meeting another incredible woman as you almost immediately is the hand of Providence. I am the luckiest person in this world. And yet I live with a pang of guilt. I have hurt your feelings. I have not been able to return your love."

"Mike, when it comes to matters of the heart, we are all helpless. Everything happens for a reason, so you ought not to feel guilty."

"You are a wise and very strong woman. I cannot thank you enough for your understanding."

"When you meet Dorothy, don't forget to kiss and hug her tight. And... I have decided to move back to India." She had barely uttered this shocking statement when she burst into tears. I was instantly rattled by her disclosure, yet had no option but to stay unflustered and offer a strong shoulder to console her. I embraced her and held her close, even as she wept incessantly. The time to part ways had never crossed my mind, and yet I could see its inevitability. We had become so used to each other, almost like a good habit, and in the midst of our multilayered personal and professional involvement, I had forgotten that our treasured association would sooner or later give way to Dorothy's reentry into my life. Meher's tears and the thought of impending separation left me speechless and with a lump in my throat. Things would change from here on, and we were clearly not ready for it.

"I'm sorry," Meher said. "I didn't mean to shock you, but I couldn't hold my tears back." She wiped her moist face with a tissue and started to take charge of her emotions. The ensuing silence was the perfect interlude for both of us to get a hold on our plummeting spirits. After all, I too had just felt the unprepared spasm of separation.

"But why do you have to return to India?" I asked, certain my expression revealed my distress.

"Mike, you will start a new life with Dorothy. And it's time I start a new life away from you."

"Meher, don't do this to me. You can't leave just because Dorothy is about to become part of my life."

"Whatever is destined will happen. If we are meant to reunite, so shall it be. If not, you and I will settle into our new lives with cherished memories of our times together. Let us please not talk about this anymore. You are very special. I can only ask you to accept and honor my decision with a smile."

"When do you intend to return to India?" I asked, more out of the acceptance she asked for than consent.

"As soon as my request for a transfer to the Mumbai office is approved."

I began to feel crushingly suffocated in her apartment. Leaving her home to get fresh air seemed the only way I could breathe normally again. Undoubtedly, I had been knocked down by Meher's decision to return to Mumbai. I had the world at my feet, and yet my world had fallen apart. The very idea of Meher parting ways with me had taken the wind out of my sails. My heart heavy, I hugged her good-bye and left.

As I drove back to my apartment, I reflected on the turn of events that had brought Meher into my life, the subsequent memorable journey, and the wretched revelation of her departure that had disrupted it all.

My emotions were running high, and I was crying on the inside. Behind my extraordinary success was the remarkable sacrifice of an exceptional woman—Dorothy. Behind my meteoric rise was the outstanding effort of an unusually supportive woman—Meher. I had never met a fascinating woman as Dorothy. I had never received such unconditional love as I had from Meher. I had lived without Dorothy for a few years, but living without Meher seemed unimaginable. Was life throwing up the biggest surprise of my existence—that hitherto unknown to me, I was deeply in love with Meher? Had facing our impending separation uncovered the immeasurable love for her that lay obscured in my deepest recesses? *Was I in love with two women at the same time?*

My state of mind could be expressed as indescribable bewilderment. The celebrated relationship coach had aided countless clients throughout the world, but oddly enough had to clear out the cobwebs in his own mind to find his way across the final frontier of his love story.

My car decided to stop at Tommy Nevin's Pub in Evanston for a quiet drink. The night was threatening to be the longest night of my life, and I had to be at someplace that could provide clarity of thought and raise my crestfallen spirits. The last time I had visited Tommy Nevin's was after I had finished writing the business plan for my resurgence as a relationship coach. Over beer, I had recounted the best "first" moments of my life. Over beer this night, I sought answers for my emotional distress.

Everything happens for a reason, so you ought not to feel guilty.

Meher's unforgettable words played again and again in my mind. Had Andrew not invited me to

Lima, I wouldn't have met Dorothy. Had I not pursued the reason behind Dorothy's unexpected exit from Andrew's life, I wouldn't have fallen in love with her. Had Dorothy not made her sacrifice and Andrew bestowed his legacy, I wouldn't have met Meher. Had Meher not been dumped by her boyfriend, she wouldn't have moved to the US. And had Meher not put her soul and heart into promoting my books and my practice, I wouldn't have become such a celebrity.

Everything happens for a reason but everything that was good, enthralling, and unexpected in my life had happened too fast, too soon. Both Dorothy and Meher were instrumental in my success. Dorothy was divinely profound, and Meher captivatingly intense. If I loved them both, whom do I choose? Did I base my decision on who I loved more or who loved me most? Whom do I hurt? If I chose wrong, would that at some point in time hurt two people even more?

A chilled beer later, a stream of cogent thoughts flowed through my more relaxed mind.

If the immediate purpose of my trip to Lima had been to inherit a legacy, the larger predestined plan had been to lead me to Dorothy. After all, how many people in this world could even think of being loved by such a lovely and discriminating person, let alone find such a profound emotional connection with that person? The beer kicked my mind in the right direction, for even though my heart acknowledged that

I was in love with two amazing women, I saw that Dorothy was my future.

I had made a decision, and I had to follow it with a trip to Lima very soon, perhaps in a few days or a week. A big surprise was awaiting Dorothy.

There was no time to waste. The next day, I bought my ticket to Lima.

The flights via Miami were full, so the next best alternative was to fly through Toronto to ensure that I reached Lima as soon as possible. My reunion with Dorothy was now merely four days away. As I printed off my ticket, I was reminded of the beautiful adage, "The love of a woman and a bottle of wine are sweet for a season but last for a time."

Nostalgia sparked my recollection of some of Dorothy's thoughtful words from her good-bye letter

I love you immensely and ask for your forgiveness to accept my selfless explanation. You may not comprehend the rationale of my good-bye, and yet I am confident that in time to come you will recognize the merit of the argument. With a heavy heart, I write this note and bid you good-bye—and to request a favor from you. Please do not meet me again until such time as you have realized your dream.

Dorothy was right about the single-minded pursuit of my goal devoid of any distractions. If she had stayed and not bid me good-bye, I would have become so wrapped up in her adoration, I would have been unable to focus on taking my relationship-coaching practice to the pinnacle of global prominence.

Equally factual was a hard-hitting reality: I had the money but nobody to prod me to move out of my old apartment. I had won the adulation of people across the world, yet I hankered for the love of a woman beside me. I had everything that money could buy, but I came home to an empty apartment. In essence, even though I had achieved it all, realized my big dream, my life had an empty space that could only be filled by Dorothy. That day, the renowned relationship coach was reminded of a cardinal truth. Attainments are very important, but when there is no beloved with whom to share them, it is like having many houses but not a single home, billions of dollars of treasure but not even a thousand dollars of happiness.

I no longer wanted to live in a place that reflected only my achievements and personality. I wanted to live in a castle of love, warmth, touch, and banter. And the lady who would create this citadel was merely ninety-six hours away from taking her first step in this direction.

A day later, I called Meher to apprise her of my imminent visit to Lima, only to get another blow.

"Let us get together again," she said. "This will be our last meeting."

"But why won't we meet again? I'll be back in Chicago with Dorothy before you return to India. I want you to meet her."

"I'm not sure if I can bear seeing both of you together. I would much rather be candid about my feelings."

There is no true love without jealousy. Meher loved me enormously, yet understandably was green-eyed. The irony of Meher's unconditional love was that she could love me wholeheartedly without expecting love in return, but it was difficult for her even to consider seeing me with another woman. I couldn't blame her for her honest remark.

We both had our acceptance issues. I could not accept the bolt from the blue that Meher and I would not meet again. She could not tolerate the sight of Dorothy and me. She might have suggested I make a trip to Lima, but she had decided she would be gone before I returned.

The mystery had been unraveled, yet I just could not believe or digest this most disconcerting news— Meher and I were hours away from our last tryst.

My gloomy silence was interrupted by Meher's perceptive yet audacious comment.

"Mike, let's not spoil what we've shared. You and I are both right from our perspectives, and we will always want the best for each other. Let us only wish each other well. Love will return to your life after a long time, and I will go back home with a lot of beautiful memories and learning. I never loved you to take Dorothy's place. I loved you only to bring joy to my heart. And remember that if we are meant to be together, it will happen."

"When can we meet?" I asked, my voice rough with my pain. Something jagged had hit my heart and mind, and I could not conceal my agony.

"No restaurant. Let's make it your place or mine," Meher replied.

"My place, considering it's your farewell party. Let me do the honors."

"Very well, tomorrow night at eight. Would that work for you?"

"Well, I have no other option, given that you will disappear on me thereafter. We will make it an early night," I said, my bitter words revealing my upset.

"Mike, this is not easy for either of us, but the best of friends someday have to part. Let's make our last evening together special. If I have ever meant anything to you, please accept my departure with a smile. That would be the best parting gift."

At that moment, her soft voice and gentle words were so precious, perhaps the most valuable since we had known each other. Such was the effect of our impending separation.

"I promise you it will be special," I said. "See you tomorrow night. And please be on time," I added, thinking of how important every minute with her now was.

"Yes, sir. Your wish is my command. I will be on time and you better look good. I'll let you go so that you can start preparing for tomorrow night."

She hung up, but I continued to stare at my phone, hoping for a last-minute miracle that would keep her in Chicago.

That night I could not sleep. Meher and I were barely hours away from saying good-bye. A farewell from her was unthinkable. We knew intimately each other's preferences, moods, strengths, and flaws. Most times, before we had even exchanged a word, she knew what I was thinking; and each time she was upset, I invariably knew my shoulder and ears were the perfect support.

Meher was a great conversationalist, and I a reasonable raconteur. She had been a good tennis player, and I an above-average golfer. She was an avid reader, and I lived on books. She enjoyed romantic comedies, and I was a movie buff. She was a communications expert, and I could coin expressions at the drop of a hat. She had traveled half the world, and I took pleasure in my own wanderlust. She was spiritual, and I believed in ubiquitous love. As if all that was not enough, she was a foodie and I enjoyed eating out... and we both loved Indian food. If somebody had to look for compatibility between two people, he or she would not have to go beyond

Meher and me. If I did not love Dorothy immeasurably, Meher and I would have become a couple.

A fantasy moment of sensual recall took me back to that night when Meher and I made love to each other. I could not stop my mind from remembering every move and act that had made our lovemaking so exceptionally gratifying.

Meher had thrown all her inhibitions to the wind because she was giving herself completely to a man she trusted implicitly and loved immensely. I had subconsciously and inadvertently reciprocated with the vigor of a man deeply in love, although my mental focus had been on her seductive body and my need to express my gratitude for all she had done for me. The melodious union of our two compatible souls had made for an astonishingly unforgettable night. Recalling that memorable night in detail kept me awake all night long.

At the crack of dawn, I hit the road for a run. The cool air energized a groggy mind and body, uplifting my somnolent spirit and stimulating me enough that my perspiring body felt better by the end of the three-mile run.

The early-morning zephyr had also kindled my imaginative brainpower as I had thought of the perfect gift for Meher to make her farewell memorable. Some interesting ideas came to the fore, but one thing was clear. The evening, the food and drink, everything must be to her taste. Why not make it an

Indian evening? Meher and I relished Indian food, and truly enjoyed Indian beer.

Some months earlier, she had given me an embroidered sky-blue kurta pajama—a traditional loose-fitting Indian shirt that falls to just below the knees and similarly loose-fitting trousers with a drawstring waist. Since I had never worn the outfit, I decided it would be the most appropriate attire for me for that evening.

By the time I finished my run, I had drawn up my agenda for the day. In the first half, a visit to Michigan Avenue to buy a necklace for Meher; and later in the afternoon, a trip to an authentic Indian restaurant on Devon Avenue to buy a scrumptious dinner. I had a stock of Indian tipple in my refrigerator, so I was well covered in the beverage segment.

A shower and breakfast later, I headed to Michigan Avenue to look for a classy necklace. Meher had a beautiful neck, and it deserved to have an exquisite necklace adorning it. I also wanted to explicitly show her that she had a very special place in my life; and just as the neck and necklace would look striking when together, our friendship bloomed in each other's presence. Additionally, I wanted to subtly send another message: please don't go. I wanted to make a last-ditch effort without putting it in words.

On Michigan Avenue, I walked into one of the most renowned jewelry stores in Chicago. After half an hour of analyzing various necklaces, I chose an elegant gold necklace with clear white diamond pendant. A small card with my handwritten message accompanied the gift package:

> *My Dear Meher,*
>
> *Please accept my token of heartfelt gratitude and adoration. This necklace truly belongs to your beautiful neck. Just as you adorned my life, this necklace is embellished with a lady's best friend, diamonds. You are my best special mate and will be immensely missed, even though I hope and pray that you stay so that you will not be missed.* ☺
>
> *Warm hugs and lots of love,*
>
> *Mike*

After I returned home with Meher's gift, I felt rather drowsy, possibly because I hadn't slept the night before. I needed to indulge in a siesta to rejuvenate my exhausted body for a very important evening. A three-hour nap recharged my lifeless disposition, and I quickly made my trip to Devon Avenue to purchase our delectable dinner, which consisted of dal makhani, paneer butter masala, bhindi fry, tandoori roti, naan, spicy samosa, and vegetable pakora. Later that night, I would reheat the gourmet delicacies when Meher and I were ready to feast on them.

The next significant task for the eventful evening was to choose the music. Of course, I picked soft and sentimental numbers. Time flew, and before I knew it was seven. An hour to go before Meher arrived at my doorstep. Despite being preoccupied with the thought of making her farewell unforgettable, a sinking feeling of loneliness had enveloped me all day long. A warm shower to wash away my plummeting mood was the fitting therapy. It worked wonders, and with fresh optimism I put on my new clothes. To my mind, the mirror did not lie that evening. I was sure I would get an admiring comment from Meher.

Precisely at eight, the musical ding-dong of my doorbell announced Meher's arrival. I opened the door and was bowled over by a bewitching vision. Meher was draped in a sparkling red sari that enhanced the understated sensual side of the traditionally attired maiden. It also made me pay a genuine compliment.

"Meher, you look absolutely stunning in a sari."

"Thank you. Mike, you look imperial. Truly, today the king of human connections could pass as a maharaja."

"For once I took you by surprise. You had no clue that I would wear this kurta pajama."

"Just as you had no idea I was going to surprise you with a sari."

"The surprises have just commenced," I said cheekily.

"I can hardly wait. Bring it on," she replied.

"For starters, would you care for some Indian beer with samosa and vegetable pakora?"

"So you are going to feed me Indian food tonight. That is so sweet of you."

"Do you mind heating up the appetizers while I get the beer?"

"With pleasure, although you will have to make sure I do not get drunk tonight."

"On the contrary, I think we should talk and drink till we get inebriated." I laughed. "I'm just kidding."

A few minutes later, we had our first sip of the chilled tipple, and then we devoured the appetizers. Meher had reserved her appetite for the evening, and I too had skipped lunch for our farewell meal.

"My apologies," I said, "but I cannot thank your former boyfriend enough. It is because of him that you and I started a friendship. Otherwise, our relationship would have largely stayed professional."

"Considering that you read my eyes and pain when we first met, I agree with your observation."

"When you return to Mumbai, do you have plans to get married?" I asked audaciously, knowing very well that I could be inviting trouble. Yet for some strange reason I wanted an answer.

"Would you be able to see me get married to a man of my choice?" she asked.

"But of course. Why would I have a problem?"

"Because you know what I know."

"And what do you know that I know as well?"

"You would not be able to see me with another man for true love gets green with envy. Mike, you and I are very similar in this aspect."

She had stated the blunt truth as if she had once again figured out what was going on in my mind. She was right. Just as she could not see me in person with Dorothy, I could not see her face-to-face with another man.

"You love two women," she went on, "and after what I'm sure was painstaking contemplation, you have made your choice."

I did not know what to say. I could neither deny nor accept her pointed comment. Instead, I changed the subject.

"Meher, you are returning to India with cutting-edge knowledge of communications practices. That will make you a much sought-after PR professional."

"I have been away for a while, so I will need to go back with an open mind in order to make a smooth transition on both the professional and personal fronts."

"If you ever want to return to the United States, you know I am just a phone call away. Not that you'll require my assistance, because you are super smart."

"I know I can always count on you. For all you know, I may be back sooner than you can imagine.

Destiny brought me here, and if my karmic connection with the US is not over, I could be back."

"I really hope that happens," I replied, and then excused myself to get a refill of vegetable pakora. I returned with a bowl of pakora in one hand and Meher's gift in the other. As she started to unwrap the package, I advanced the CD so that the soul-stirring song "Seasons in the Sun" began playing in the background.

She gasped with delight when she saw my gift. "Mike, this necklace is the best gift I've ever received from anybody in my life, and your note is very touching. I will treasure these more than anything else I possess. Thank you." She planted a sweet kiss on my cheek.

"Meher, you will be greatly missed. You only have to listen to these lyrics to know exactly how I feel at this moment." I softly sang along, "'Goodbye to you, my trusted friend…'"

Meher and I remained silent until the end of the poignant song. What did not remain quiet were our emotion-filled eyes, which stayed fixed on each other. Separation and love did not need words to convey the mélange of sentiments—pain, hollowness, and fondness. Barely had "Seasons in the Sun" ended that another captivating song began to play, from the film *Dirty Dancing*. I immediately asked her for a dance. We began to slow dance and held each other close. Romance was the farthest thing on our mind.

A few minutes into our dance, I kissed her forehead. She hugged me tight as if she did not want to leave, and the next thing we knew, we had tears in our eyes. Crying together, making no attempt to wipe each other's tears or change each other's mind, we knew the final leg of our amazing journey together was about to end. We were weeping together but could not stay together. We knew the last touch, the last hug, and the last glimpse were the only significant highlights of that cheerless night. No more face-to-face conversations, disagreements, fights, and smiles. No more meaningful exchanges. No more drinks and meals together. No more work and book promotion together. From that moment on, nothing mundane mattered that evening. The music, the beer, the appetizers, and the dinner had already been forgotten.

Meher and I closed our eyes and held hands for a while in quietude. For once we did not wish to talk to each other; we just wanted to feel the vibes we had shared all these years. An unusual and deep-rooted friendship was being relived in silence and through closed eyes. Slowly but surely, laughter displaced the tears as we opened our eyes and broke our silence to recount our squabbles that did not count anymore. An air of levity enveloped the living room, even though deep down, we both were still blue.

"Mike, please make sure that the next book you write has a chapter titled 'Never Argue with a Woman When She Is Right or Smarter Than You.' And please ensure that argumentative men like you read the chapter a few times over."

"That is a promise, but only if you give your word that the next time you argue with a wise man, you will remember to think of wise Mike," I replied playfully.

The lighthearted banter continued for almost an hour, only to have it abruptly end when Meher excused herself. She reappeared a few minutes later wearing the elegant necklace around her beautiful neck, looking astonishingly lovely in the prized piece of jewelry. I could never repay her for her invaluable role in my spectacular climb, but I could make certain that no other neck would look as lovely as Meher's when she sported the chic necklace. She deserved a lot more, but I was not rich enough to give Meher what she truly desired.

"Mike, you have a very fine taste in jewelry. You sure know how to make a woman feel special and wanted."

"And you sure know how to create a void in my life," I said without hesitation, giving vent to my repressed feelings.

"Why would you feel like that? Dorothy is about to return in your life."

"Because I really love you and I cannot see you

go," I said reflexively, making the most unexpected candid admission.

"You love me immensely, yet you have decided to return to Dorothy. I can never take her place, and I am brave enough to accept that. It's time you accept the news of my imminent departure," Meher retorted.

There was an uneasy silence between us. A minute later, a visibly upset Meher got up from the couch and said, "I am sorry, but I think it's time for me to leave. Thank you for the lovely evening, the gift, your cherished friendship, and the memorable times together. I will miss you. God bless you and good luck in your new life with Dorothy."

I caught her hand and held it tight. Her eyes were moist with tears, and she would not look at me. I realized it was the end of a unique relationship. I knew the time had once again come for the best of friends to part. I could not hold her back. It was time to let go. She walked away with tears on her face, and I stayed back with a heavy heart.

ELEVEN

Two days later, I flew out of Chicago en route to Lima via Toronto. The flight landed at Jorge Chávez International Airport at 8:40 a.m. A prebooked cab was waiting at the airport to take me to Del Pilar Miraflores Hotel. I had stayed there on my last trip to Lima and decided to enjoy the hospitality of the hotel again. The reception desk at the hotel was gracious enough to grant me the same sixth floor room I'd had the last time around. For some reason, I felt it was the luckiest hotel room of my life, since my search for and subsequent pursuit of Dorothy had started from that room.

Post shower, I left the hotel asked a waiting taxi-cab to head in the direction of Dorothy's apartment. The short drive should have taken twenty minutes, but we got caught up in sporadic traffic conges-tion, making it seem like the longest drive of my life. With every passing minute, the nervous exhilaration within me made my hands fidget and my legs shake. I had never been so edgy and impatient; I was struggling to stay composed. I just could not wait any longer to hug Dorothy. Finally, thirty-five minutes later, the cabbie made it to her apartment.

It seemed like yesterday when Dorothy and I had taken a cab together to her home from the panoramic Larcomar. I took a deep breath and walked into the lobby of the apartment building, where I was informed at the reception that Dorothy was not at home. They did not know when she would be back. I could have waited in the lobby for her to return, but I was not prepared to twiddle my thumbs. I had to find her immediately, but how and where would I do that? Realizing my restiveness was not helping me at all, I sat in a chair, closed my eyes, and dropped into a meditative state. Shortly thereafter my inner voice spoke: *Mike, you will find her at Larcomar.* It was the very place I had first met Dorothy. I hurried back outside. A car was waiting, a service for residents and guests of the apartment complex, and I asked the chauffeur to drive me there.

The driver took precisely twenty-eight minutes to reach Larcomar. I literally leaped out of the car and sprinted toward La Dama Juana, the restaurant where I had first met Dorothy. Not a soul resembling her was to be seen in the restaurant. No sooner had my gaze searched all four corners of La Dama

Juana, than I rushed out to search for Dorothy at other restaurants and stores at Larcomar. Forty minutes of futile searching was enough to convince me that in my fervent excitement, I had been too quick to listen to my inner voice. Dorothy must have been someplace else, and it was time to go back to her apartment building and patiently wait in the lobby for her return.

Just as I was getting ready to leave Larcomar, I saw a comely woman walk out of the restroom. Wonder of wonders it was Dorothy. *Yes*, it was my Dorothy. I had looked everywhere, only to find her appear out of nowhere. I could not hold back my excitement as I shouted, "Dorothy, my love, I am back for you. I have kept my promise."

Dorothy hugged me tight and buried her face in my chest. She and I did not exchange a word as I cuddled her in my arms. She looked up at me, unable to hold back her tears of joy, and I could not take my eyes off her. To my ears, our silence was the symphony of a blissful reunion. The journey to fame and acclaim had ended, and a new journey of love and togetherness was about to commence. We would now live with each other, and I would shower on Dorothy the endless love she had missed out on all these years because of me. Not an iota of the clamor around us mattered. Our hearts were beating in sync, connected by a deep, spiritual love that made the outward façade of words and actions inconsequential. At that moment, we had become one.

Still without speaking, we walked to a waiting taxi, which drove us to her abode. Very little had changed in her elegant seventh floor apartment—the reproduction of the eternal *Mona Lisa*, the baby grand piano, the embellished golden silk curtains, the black leather couch, Persian carpets, and mahogany bookcase still decorated the living room. The only noticeable additions were Andrew's framed picture and my books, placed on the coffee table beside the couch. The two men she loved most were a part of her life and home.

Dorothy's first words since we had met were wonderfully normal. "Mike, you're looking good. Would you like an equally good cup of coffee?"

"Thank you. I would, as long as the cup of coffee looks as attractive and smells as aromatic as you." I was enraptured by both her age-defying, eye-catching beauty and the delicate fragrance that surrounded her.

Shortly thereafter, Dorothy appeared with two cups of aromatic coffee and a plate of cheese sandwiches. She had possibly sensed I had skipped breakfast and was hungry. Over coffee and sandwiches, I had a lot to tell her about my journey from when I had left Lima before to unimaginable success. But before that, I wanted to know of her well-being, particularly after Andrew's death. It may have taken a toll on her, yet I was hoping that with the passage of time, Dorothy had recovered from the tragedy.

"You look more attractive than before," I said. "Does that mean you are in a tranquil place?"

"You really want to know if I've recovered from Andrew's loss," she said. "It did hurt a lot, and it would have been worse had I not seen him before he died. While my intention to make an unexpected exit from his life was noble, I would never have been able to forgive myself had he passed away without us seeing each other one last time. He and I owe you the world. His bestowing his rich legacy on you has been more than duly compensated by your grand gesture to track me down to fulfill a dying man's last wish. Thank you, Mike." She grasped my hands in gratitude. Her modesty was showing up one more time. She was one of the biggest reasons behind Andrew's and my illustrious careers, yet she was grateful for a minor initiative on my part that had not been completely altruistic.

"You don't have to thank me." I said. "A small effort to bring Andrew and you together was not a completely selfless act."

"Andrew will always have a special place in my heart."

I was glad to hear that Andrew had an uncommon corner in Dorothy's heart that nobody else could occupy. I had not an iota of envy toward Andrew. On the contrary, I better understood the nature and depth of Andrew and Dorothy's relationship for I was in the same boat with Meher. I loved Dorothy immensely, yet Meher and our association was unforgettable.

"Mike," Dorothy went on, "ever since your renaissance, I followed every article, report, and interview that featured you. However, I'm eager to get your version of your story. Tell me all, every small detail that transpired to make you so big upon your return to the States."

I had known Dorothy would ask me about the events that led to my global acclaim and I would have to reveal Meher's in my rapid climb. The test of my character would depend upon either selective disclosure or complete revelation of Meher and my unique relationship. I chose the latter, honest admission of the evolution of our relationship. I knew Dorothy would understand because she too had loved more than one person.

I began my story with my flight from Lima to Miami, when I had recorded in my laptop the profound and meaningful insights Dorothy and Andrew had so generously provided, and concluded it with the poignant farewell to Meher. In between, I gave a detailed account of the events that involved the repositioning, resurrection, and growing success of my relationship-coaching practice, spurred by Meher's PR ingenuity, painstaking effort, and intimate involvement. I told Dorothy about the remarkable global recognition of my novel *The Suitable*

Inheritor; and how through all of this, I always felt her presence around me and longed for the day when I could reunite with her. And I also articulated how Meher had comforted me when I learned of Andrew's death, and that we had shared a memorable night of physical gratification.

As if this was not enough, I candidly confessed to loving two women at the same time. Meher and I had recognized that everything happens for a reason, and perhaps our separation was imperative for us to move on to where we truly belonged. Since I had reached the pinnacle of my goal, it was time for me to return to Lima and Meher to India.

Dorothy intently listened to every word of my in-depth narrative. She did not interrupt me once or ask any questions. At the end of the story, she moved closer, hugged me, and started to gently rub my back. A few minutes later she said, "Mike, you are an honest man. It requires a backbone to make such an open and descriptive disclosure. Andrew spotted you as the inheritor of his legacy, and he was exactly right."

At that moment I felt light, almost weightless, after baring all the intricate and intimate particulars that Meher and I had shared between ourselves. It was imperative for Dorothy to know about this incredible woman from India, even as it was equally important for me to be truthful in my own esteem. I could live with the unpleasant consequences of

Dorothy being deeply offended by my relationship with Meher, but I could not live with the biggest fib of my life, by keeping Meher and our lovemaking a secret known only to God.

"Mike, I would like to say something important, and until I finish, I would ask you not to interject."

"I promise not to butt in," I replied.

"You love Meher deeply. You mentioned her name over fifty times. You intimately know each other's moods, strengths, flaws, and interests. You also know very well that had she not put her soul into promoting your practice and your books, you would not have become such a well-known person. You are well aware that she gave her body, mind, and spirit entirely to you knowing, her love for you would stay unrequited. You have known Meher for only a short amount of time, yet it feels as if you have known her all your life. You just told me that on many occasions, she knew what was going on in your mind even before a word had been exchanged between the two of you. You have compatible inter-ests—sports, books, movies, travel, and more. You said that she's 'scorching hot,' and that drew you to her time and again. You were rattled by her decision to relocate and felt an unexpected spasm of sepa-ration. You eloquently verbalized that she and you cried together inconsolably, and felt a mélange of pain, hollowness, and fondness. You confessed that the king of human connections had the world at his feet, and yet his world had fallen apart. To my mind, you are subconsciously mired in the biggest dilemma of your life: Is Dorothy's sacrifice greater than the zealous efforts of an extremely supportive and loving Meher? In the answer to this simple question lies the secret and solution to your happy future."

In one fell swoop she had brought out the deep-rooted reality I had kept buried and locked away—my intense love for Meher was being obscured because of the burden of a selfless, once-in-a-lifetime act made by an exceptional woman. Dorothy had made my mind-boggling quandary appear small, and she had expressed it without difficulty, heartache, or regret.

"My dear, what are you thinking?" she said. "You have achieved great things, all you wanted, without my physical presence, but I cannot imagine you thriving without Meher at your side. There are two kinds of love, spiritual love and physical love. You and I are deeply connected through a spiritual love that is beyond the concept of physical presence or shared expectations. Our love for each other is and will remain ubiquitous. Our union is beyond material expectations or bodily gratification. It is a communion of mind and spirit. We are deeply in love and will always love each other, irrespective of whether you stay with me or go to Meher. On the contrary, you and Meher are intensely connected through a physical love driven by your high compatibility, similar interests, need for each other's presence, and an overwhelming attraction for each other. You too have a spiritual connection with Meher, because you feel you have known each other all your lives, but the material attachment is more overpowering. The very thought of physical separation flustered both of you. It was unimaginable.

Let me now help you choose between sacrifice and support. I have sacrificed, but the sacrifice was not the most potent catalyst in your drive to success. Yes, in my sacrifice there was a silent support that might have left you unencumbered to pursue your ambition, but without the amazing efforts from an unusually supportive woman such as Meher, you would not have gotten anywhere close to international prominence. Sacrifice may come with silent, fervent, or financial support, but unusual support invariably comes with passionate commitment and willing sacrifice. So Meher's support is bigger than my sacrifice."

She paused to sip her coffee and eat a few bites of a cheese sandwich. I could not stop looking at her deferentially. After all, how many people can negate their invaluable contribution and make it appear trivial? Dorothy truly had reached an elevated state of mind, a spiritual enlightenment at a level far higher than I could ever attain.

"Mike, I want you to do me another favor. Close your eyes and dig deep. You will most certainly see the face of the woman who appeared in your dream and led you to the Pacific Ocean."

Baffled, I did as she asked and shut my eyes in order to see. She asked me to remain quiet and not worry about passing thoughts. I needed to go within, deep inside, as deep as I could to permeate my inner recesses. Slowly but surely the noise of my thoughts dissipated, and what lingered was silence and serenity. A blurred image began to emerge. I did not try to decipher the fuzzy picture, but stayed tranquil and still. Bit by bit, the image got clearer, and I saw a woman dressed in white walking hand in hand with a man toward a gigantic ocean. I stayed calm, only to see seconds later the face of the woman in white. *It was not Dorothy, it was Meher.* The mystery of the dream woman was resolved.

Slowly, I opened my eyes to the most compassionate, giving, and beautiful woman in the world—Dorothy, who was sitting right in front of me. Her ethereal smile said it all. She knew that my inner recesses had caught a glimpse of Meher's face. No more questions remained unanswered. There were no apologies or explanations to offer, no more promises to be made, no more stories to share. There was no more longing for Dorothy's physical presence. We just had to close our eyes and we could feel each other's presence. Such was the depth of our ubiquitous love.

"Mike," Dorothy said, still gazing at me, "if I

were you, I would stop Meher right away. Don't lose a moment."

I grasped her hands. "Dorothy, I can't thank you enough for all what you have done for me. I will always love you dearly."

"We love each other as few can, and we have no competitors. We are unique. We are one and will always remain deeply connected. For most, separation means loss, grief, and tears. For us, it is a communion of our minds and spirits. You and I are always with each other, twenty-four seven."

"Andrew bequeathed a legacy to me. Now you have conferred an inheritance too, a dimension of togetherness unknown to those who are in love."

So once again in Lima, I had received an inheritance. This time I would use my bequest to stay in eternal love with Dorothy and passionate love with Meher. Dorothy and I indulged in a warm soul hug. No tears, no good-bye, and no remorse. Everything happens for a reason. Dorothy had entered my life to become a soul mate, and Meher to become a special mate. Destiny had brought both of these women to me, and destiny would not separate us.

As I took a cab to Larcomar, I sent a text message to Meher: *I love you immensely and I'm sorry for hurting you. Please do not go back. I will return very soon… to be with you forever.*

Her reply came promptly. *What happened in Lima? What made you change your mind?*

A new inheritance bequeathed by Dorothy. She made it happen.

Another sacrifice? That is not fair to her.

No sacrifice, guilt or promise, I texted. *Only a new facet of love and togetherness.*

I miss you more than anything. Can't imagine living without you.

You don't have too. I will be back soon and upon arrival, I want to see you in a sari," I texted back.

I put my phone away since I had arrived at Larcomar. I wanted to express my gratitude in solitude to the magnificent Pacific Ocean. As I soaked in the magnificent view of the ocean, I looked back over the past few years with marvel. It had started with an uncharacteristic early-morning dream in Chicago—a lady dressed in white led me to the beautiful Pacific Ocean and whispered in my ear, "The ethereal ocean will now bring a wave of graces your way. Keep your inner door open to receive the special graces and discover your true destiny."

And today was truly the day when I had received the largest inheritance of my life. I had found my destiny—true love.

GRATITUDE

THIS NOVEL WOULD not exist without the grace of God, my source and strength. Thank you for *inspiring me to write.*

All writers need allies. These are mine. Foremost, I owe my wife and chief proofreader, Madhur, a greater debt than I can express. An accomplished psychologist, gifted writer, and avid reader of fiction, she carefully read over my manuscript at various stages and offered many invaluable suggestions. Beyond her endless patience, her willingness to drop everything and read when I needed her discerning eye, and her candid comments, she has given me the greatest of gifts: her generous involvement.

My niece Natasha and my nephews Ajay, Karan, Shaan, and Seth are an endless source of wonder and pride. The power of their imagination, curiosity, energy, optimism, and innocence fuels my creative fire. They have taught me to be fearless and discard what people around me are saying to be a better writer and creative professional.

A big thank you to my in-laws, Jyotsna and Dr. Suraj Sancheti, for treating me like a son and for their support, love, and understanding.

I am indebted to my brother-in-law, Vivek Mehta, for encouraging me to write my first book in 2006. That was the turning point in my creative career.

A special nod of gratitude goes to Elizabeth Barrett. She did a fantastic job as an editor and held my feet to the fire time after time, making for a much better finished product.

I am grateful to Sangeeta Mehta of Mehta Book Editing, New York. Unfailingly generous with her time and publishing advice, she went out of her way to suggest leads and respond to my queries.

With all the gratitude I can summon, I would like to thank my former colleagues who suggested I write a novel. Their persistence forced me to complete the most important writing project of my life. Thank you:

Jori Lynne Ortegon, Long Pineda, Tiodita Mori, Tanwi Tiwary, Bong Roxas, Diwakar Ram B, Mathew Sangma, Venkateswaran SS, and Sambit Lenka.

My deep appreciation goes to Ilaxi Patel, Shefali Lahoti, Sheela Dalal, Nimisha Bajaj Jaipuria, Abhilasha Agarwal, Vandana Suri, Renee Appert, Suzie Housley, Pamela Davis, Katie Hulgrave

McNaughton, Amisha Shah, Chelly Long, Niya Moon, Lindsey Jozefiak, Kritika Pandey Gower, Seema Sudan, Ajay Singh Mehta, Dinesh Pagaria, Anup Samanta, Kyle Parker, and Christopher Rathje for your deep encouragement to spur my writing voice and creativity. My journey as a writer has been enriched because of your valuable insights

Finally, I offer my appreciation and gratitude to you, the reader. I hope you find the novel worthwhile. Please feel free to engage in a conversation with me about life and relationships by writing to pushpendramehtausa@gmail.com

Pushpendra Mehta
Atlanta, Georgia

About the Author

PUSHPENDRA MEHTA IS the author of the books *Win the Battles of Life & Relationships* and *Tomorrow's Young Achievers*, which have earned him an internationally loyal readership. The richness of his experience comes from having donned diverse roles—writer, marketer, consultant, and entrepreneur. He considers exposure to disparate people, places, and situations his biggest asset. Interaction with the wealthy and successful, and the strugglers and powerless, both in the East and the West, has enriched his understanding of human behavior, life, and relationships. Pushpendra was raised in India and now lives in Atlanta, Georgia. He is an alumnus of Northwestern University and Sydenham College of Commerce & Economics.

pushpendramehtausa@gmail.com
Facebook.com/AuthorPushpendraMehta
Twitter @mehtapush

Made in the USA
Lexington, KY
02 April 2016